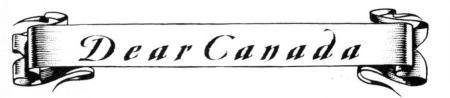

A Country of Our Own

✧

The Confederation Diary of Rosie Dunn

BY KARLEEN BRADFORD

Scholastic Canada Ltd.

Ottawa, Province of Canada,
1866

Sunday, April 29ᵗʰ, 1866
Québec City, Province of Canada

My life is about to be turned upside down.

When we got home from Mass this noon, we found Mary Margaret here. Not too unusual that, as she gets every other Sunday off from the Bradleys', but what was unusual was that she was humped over the kitchen table in floods of tears. Mary Margaret almost never weeps. She is usually obnoxiously cheerful. The last time I saw her cry was when she and Donny Malone fell out three months ago. I thought she was over it by now, but sure, hasn't everything gone and changed!

At first no amount of encouragement from Mam could get her to say a word, but finally I got exasperated and blurted out, "Fine then, weep if you must, but could we not sit down to our dinner before it gets burned to a crisp?"

Mam glared at me as if I were very cold-hearted indeed, but Da and the little ones looked relieved, Paddy in particular. He does like his food.

Mary Margaret gave me a fierce look, but stopped her weeping.

"You'd be devastated too, Rosie Dunn, if you were in the fix I am," she said.

She gave a huge hiccup and burst into tears again. Mam patted her on the back — I would have given her a good shake — and she began to explain. Once she got started it seemed like she'd never stop, and the words poured out fast and furious. I can't begin to write down everything she said, but the gist of it, at first, was that she and Donny had made up and their engagement was back on.

You would think that would be good news, but it is not. Given that Queen Victoria chose Ottawa to be the capital of the Province of Canada, the Bradleys must move to Ottawa now with all the other civil servants. After Mary Margaret's falling out with Donny, she was mad keen to go with them and get away from here, even though Ottawa is said to be a horrible town away out in the middle of nowhere — nothing more than mud and sawmills — but now that they have made up, she plans to wed Donny this summer and she is adamant that she will not go with the Bradleys.

They are to leave next week, and Missus Bradley is furious with her for changing her mind at such short notice. They do have another maid, but Mary Margaret says that she is a horrible snob and she flatly refused to go right from the start. She already has another position waiting for her. That will leave the family with no maidservants at all — something Missus Bradley is obviously not used to.

Now this is the part that has stunned me past words. Mary Margaret's solution to this problem is that I should take her place with the Bradleys and go with them to Ottawa! And the worst thing is that Mam and Da are considering it! I started to protest but Mam just said I should save my breath to cool my porridge. "You'll do what you're told, me lady," she said in that tone of voice of hers that brooks no argument.

Even though I'm thirteen and I knew I would have to leave school and go into service next year — there are three younger than me to feed and clothe, after all, and I have to do my part — I never thought it would happen so soon. I love school. And Miss Edwards says I'm one of her best students. She it was who started me writing in this journal.

"You have a good hand with writing," she said.

But now to have to leave it all and go so far away! I can't even imagine it. How would Mam manage without me?

Later

Worse and worse! Mary Margaret is to take me back with her tomorrow, as Missus Bradley wants to look me over! Mam rinsed the spots out of one of Mary Margaret's old dresses for me to wear and pressed it with the flatirons. It is only a little too long for me, so I was set to shortening it, which I am supposed to be doing now. I've escaped to my corner in the children's room and am taking advantage of the fact that the rest of the family are at supper to write in this journal. My supper sits cold and abandoned beside me. Who could possibly think of eating in such a dire situation?

I don't even know for certain that Missus Bradley will agree to taking me on, so I needn't pack yet, but one thing is certain — if she does, this journal goes with me. Just as Mary Margaret will not be separated from Donny, I will not be separated from this journal. It is my last tie to Miss Edwards and school, and it is my best friend. In this noisy, rambunctious household it is

Bridget crept into the room just now, looking so upset and worried that I had to leave off writing and comfort her. She must have overheard Mam and Da talking of my leaving. Of the three younger children, she is the one who depends on me the most. I managed to reassure her, but truly, how will she get on without me? How can I keep calm myself when I am terrified even at the thought of meeting Missus Bradley? What will she think of me?

Monday, April 30th, 1866

Oh, I am not happy about this.

Mary Margaret and I set off right after breakfast. After Mary Margaret's breakfast, I should say, because in spite of Mam's urging me to keep my strength up this morning, I still could not force a bite down my throat. Maybe I should have. It might have given me courage as well as strength. I'm afraid I did not make too good an impression. I can hardly bear to write down what happened, but journals are for telling the truth in, so write it down I must.

We arrived at the Bradley house and that was the beginning of my troubles. I had no idea the house would be so grand. It's on a lovely wide street with trees on both sides, and there's a garden in the front and another in the back. And not a little kitchen garden like we have, but a vast expanse of grass, all bordered with flowers. The grass seems quite useless to me, but the flowers are lovely. And the house itself! Narrow, perhaps, but three full stories high. I was frightened before I even stepped into it. Then I made my first mistake. I started up the path to the door, but Mary Margaret grabbed me by the elbow and yanked me back.

"Not the front door, you ninny," she hissed at me. "We use the servants' door around the back."

But it was too late. Before we had a chance to retreat, the door opened and the snobby maidservant herself looked out.

"Back entrance, if you please," she sniffed at us, and slammed the door in our faces.

Mary Margaret flushed bright red and pulled me away so roughly that I can feel the sore spot on my arm still. I tried to apologize, but she just shushed me and told me to be quiet and do what she told me to do. Then we went around to the back and the same haughty maidservant opened the door to our knock.

"The Missus is waiting in the drawing room," she said. It sounded like she was talking through her nose, and the way she pronounced "drawing room," I couldn't understand what she was saying. "Draaahin' rhum" it sounded like. And I didn't know what a draaahin' rhum was, anyway, but Mary Margaret just gave me a quick look and led the way. Unfortunately, I hadn't hemmed the dress quite short enough and I almost tripped over it. I caught myself just in time, but earned another glare from Mary Margaret.

You would think she would be a bit nicer to me. After all, it's a great favour she's asking of me, it is. Still, that's Mary Margaret for you. Bossy-boots, I call her.

But not out loud.

We went down a narrow hall. I walked behind Mary Margaret, doing my best to settle the butterflies in my stomach and keep looking neat. Suddenly there was a great scraping noise and I looked up to see a monster roaring down the hall at me. I forgot all about neat, and screamed. The monster slid to a stop in front of me and began to lick my face with a sloppy red tongue. It was only then that I realized it was just a dog, but what a dog! It stood nearly as high as me, not that I'm that tall. Still, I'm usually taller than a dog.

In my panic I lost my footing and to my utter humiliation this time I did slip — and fell flat onto the floor. At that moment a gentleman appeared and loomed over me.

"What have we here?" he boomed out.

I wanted to crawl into a hole and die. I think Mary Margaret would have been happy to help me do it.

"Please, sir," she squeaked out, not sounding like her usual bossy self at all, "it's my sister, sir. Come for her interview with the Missus."

The man made a kind of harrumphing noise, then ignored me completely and strode on out the front door, leaving me sitting on the floor, utterly humiliated. Thank goodness the dog romped out after him.

Mary Margaret yanked me to my feet. "Look at you," she scolded. "You're a fine mess now, you are."

And indeed I was, but it was too late to do anything about it. We heard a voice calling from the draaahin' ruhm, and we had to go in.

Missus Bradley was sitting on a beautiful red settee. When I got closer I could see that it was velvet! I would have loved to pat it, but Mary Margaret would probably have murdered me if I tried. As it was, I could not for the life of me help gawking around the room. It was the prettiest room I have ever seen. The furniture was all covered in silks and more velvet. There were little tables in the corners whose only purpose seemed to be to hold vases of flowers. Another table in front of Missus Bradley held a teapot and cups and saucers of the purest white, with tiny little blue forget-me-not flowers on them.

I lost myself drinking it all in until Mary Margaret poked me in the side with her elbow and hissed again at me to close my mouth.

"So you are Rosie," Missus Bradley said.

I couldn't seem to make my tongue work, so I just bobbed a kind of curtsy and nodded.

"Mary Margaret says you would like to come in her place," Missus Bradley said.

"Oh, no!" I blurted out, and Mary Margaret gave me another poke, so hard that I squealed in pain.

"I mean, yes!" I cried, but truly, there is no "like" about it.

I don't even remember too much of what else was said, but I do remember how annoyed Missus Bradley was with Mary Margaret.

"It is really too bad of you, changing your mind like that," she said to her, "but there is no time to find someone else, so I suppose we will have to make do with your sister."

"Make do" with me, indeed. I was so furious that I could feel my face turn as red as a beet, but a pinch from Mary Margaret forced me to hold my tongue.

Thank goodness the maidservant will not be going. Their cook is not going, either, as they intend to hire a new one there, so at first it is just to be me and the master's manservant, James. I expect he will be just as haughty as the maid, but perhaps I won't have too much to do with him.

Oh, yes. And the dog is going. Brutus, his name is. It suits him.

Friday, May 4th, 1866

Mam is beside herself, trying to get me ready to go, and she has kept me so busy I haven't been able to write a word in this journal. She is determined that I shall make a good showing and not look poorly. She is trying to get my clothing in order, but I fear there is not much to work on. I have but one everyday cotton dress and a good linsey-woolsey for Sunday church, and now the old dress of Mary Margaret's that I shortened. Mam is washing it and my everyday dress and sponging and airing out the Sunday one as I write this, so I am confined to the children's room and enveloped in Mary Margaret's wrapper. With strict instructions from Mary Margaret not to soil it on pain of death, but as I must black my boots, I am in mortal fear. I think I will remove the wrapper and do the blacking in my shift. I hope none of the little ones will come in and find me in such a state.

The little ones! I can't stop thinking about leaving them now that all is settled. Most times I scold them more than I praise them, but now I find myself wanting to do nothing but hug and kiss them. Even little Paddy, who is never clean and always sticky. How often have I reproached him for his untidiness? I regret every word.

And Bridget, with the sweetest smile in the world. Mam says I spoil her, but how can I help it? Who will spoil her after I go? Not Mam, who is so busy she doesn't have the time for it, no matter how much she loves us. Besides, Mam doesn't believe in spoiling children. Not even Eileen, who's as messy as Paddy, twice as wild, and the bane of my life — or so I have always thought. But now, suddenly, I realize how much I will miss her noise and the sound of her laughter.

And not to smell Da's pipe of an evening before the fire. Not to help Mam with the bread-making and the sweeping and the cleaning and the washing of all those little hands and faces . . .

How can I bear it?

When I went to take my leave of Miss Edwards and tell her where I was going, she seemed as upset about me leaving school as I was. Then she put her arm around me and said, "But just think, Rosie, you'll be right in the middle of things in Ottawa. This is such an important time in our history now that our leaders are talking about the confederation of our provinces."

I think she was just trying to make me feel better, but then she asked me if I thought there would be any chance of my going back to school in Ottawa and I had to say no, and that made me feel even worse. I will be working full time so my school days are over. I am supposed to be grown up now.

Supposed to be grown up or not, here I am clutching my old rag doll, Meggy, to me. I will hide her in my bundle before the others see me and tease me for hanging on to such a childish thing. Indeed, Eileen has already declared herself too old for dolls and she is two years younger than I. But I love this old doll as much as I love my journal. She will be my secret companion when I get too lonely.

Tuesday, May 8th, 1866

I said my prayers tonight with dear little Bridget for the last time. We leave tomorrow. Tomorrow! I cannot bear to think about it.

Monday, May 14th, 1866
Ottawa, Province of Canada

We are here. At last I have I have a moment to scribble in this journal, but where to start? I am in a different world. At least I have a corner to myself where I can write in private. It is behind the kitchen and not much bigger than a broom closet, but as I am the only maidservant, I have it all to myself. James has his own quarters in the back. I have a straw tick and a pillow, and the quilt that

Grandmam made. I am sitting on my bed wrapped up in the quilt while I'm writing, and sniffing the smells it still holds of Mam and cooking and home! Meggy is tucked in beside me. I think I might well die from loneliness.

I cannot bring myself to write more now. Perhaps tomorrow.

Tuesday, May 15th, 1866

It is very late. The house is all abed and sleeping. I have only a stub of a candle, but I will try to recount at least a little of our journey here. It was so long! We left last Wednesday evening on the overnight train to Montreal. Of the parting, I can only say that it broke my heart. The little ones clung to me and wept. Da gave me a hug that would crush a bear.

"Sure, I've great faith in ye, Rosie me girl," Mam said, hugging me as well, and she's not usually much of a one for hugs. "Ye'll do well, I know it." She tried to sound positive, but her mouth trembled. I could see it.

Mary Margaret was in as great a flood of tears as the little ones. She hugged me over and over and kept saying, "Thank, you, Rosie. Thank you."

For her sake more than any other, I managed to keep from crying myself. She is happier than I have ever seen her and has already set the date when she and Donny are to be wed. How can I not be glad for her?

Da helped me carry my bundle to the ferry that would take us across the river to the train station at Pointe Levi. The Bradleys drove up in a smart pony trap just as we arrived, with James following in a wagon with a great quantity of luggage, even though most of their furniture and possessions had already been sent on ahead.

And the dog. Slobbering as usual and looking ridiculously happy. I don't think the beast has a brain in its head. I stood at the railing of the ferry all the way across, looking back. Da waved until we were out of sight and then I could not hold back the tears any longer. Fortunately, the Bradleys were sitting at the other end of the boat and did not notice.

There wasn't much time to grieve, though, as when we got off the ferry and reached the train station, the locomotive was already pulling in with a great shrieking of whistles and blowing of steam. All of a sudden everything was noise and confusion.

The Bradleys rode in a sleeper car. I was shown into a coach. James was told to see to the luggage and take the dog to a car at the end of the train, but as he led him away, the fool dog seemed to realize what was going on and of course locked his feet and balked. The last I saw of him, James was dragging him down the length of the platform. I am not certain exactly where they rode, but I could see James was none too pleased about it. James is almost as haughty as that maidservant and has not seen fit to address a word to me yet.

My candle is guttering out. I will write about that horrible journey tomorrow.

Wednesday, May 16th, 1866

I do not think I care much for the train as a mode of transportation. It was hot and stuffy in the compartment, but when I opened a window to get a breath of air, the wind blew a gust of soot and cinders back from the locomotive's smokestack and right into my face. I had to shut the window again immediately. So I just stared out through the dirty glass until the sun set and all I could see was my own reflection. With each passing moment I knew that I was getting farther and farther away from everyone that I loved. What were they all doing now, I wondered. Were their lives going on just as usual, while mine was being wrenched apart so cruelly? Did Mam remember to make certain Bridget had her warm coat on? The weather is chilly for May and Bridget takes cold so easily.

That was a miserable night. I felt so strange and alone in that car. The chattering of all the other people gradually faded away, to be replaced by snores, but I couldn't sleep. By the time we pulled into Montreal the next morning I was almost faint with exhaustion, but our trip was far from over.

In Montreal, we had to rush to make the change onto another train. I shared a compartment with

Mister and Missus Bradley on that one. Missus Bradley had a basket with provisions and she offered to share them with me, but I felt so strange and awkward in her presence, not to mention Mister Bradley's, that I said I was not hungry. Mam had provided me with bread and cheese in my bundle, and I managed a nibble of that at one of the stops when Missus and Mister Bradley got off the train to walk on the platform. But I had spoken truly. I really wasn't hungry. I was too tired and miserable to think of food.

We arrived at Prescott in the afternoon. We had more time there, and Mister Bradley was able to check on James and the dog and their baggage. Then we left for Ottawa on yet another train in the early evening, and arrived here well after 9 o'clock. In spite of the late hour, there were people everywhere, and everyone seemed to be in a raging hurry to be elsewhere. The air was heavy with a horrible smell of smoke. Mister Bradley hurried Missus Bradley off, but I was jostled and bumped on all sides. Then James appeared with the dog, and to my horror didn't he give me its rope to hang on to while he organized the luggage. I stood as still as I could and tried not to look at the beast, but it was determined to follow Mister Bradley and kept tugging after him. In spite of myself, I was pulled down the platform until I was right up beside the master. He was not pleased.

"You should stay out of the way, Rosie," he said, "until we have everything put to right."

I just muttered a "Yes, sir," and tried to yank Brutus away, but that infernal dog was having none of it. It was like trying to move one of the train cars themselves. Fortunately, a carriage pulled by two fine black horses pulled up and we all piled into it, including Brutus, who sat squashed up against my legs and drooled all over my best dress.

When we pulled up in front of the house that was to be the Bradleys', I could not believe my eyes. It is a very modest wooden building, with but two floors and a garret of sorts. It sits right on the street, if street it can be called. The road is an unpaved sea of mud. We were all so tired by that time that we wanted nothing more than to fall into bed. I helped Missus Bradley unpack some linens and I made up their bed, then I bundled myself into my little room and finally fell asleep.

How to describe this house? It is as unlike the grand house the Bradleys occupied in Québec City as it is possible to be. There is no garden to speak of and it sits bare and ugly all by itself. The next nearest house is farther down the street and is no better. I could see Missus Bradley's face fall when she got her first look at it. Inside, all was cold and damp and dark, and very unwelcoming. It is so much smaller than the Québec house. The furniture had arrived and was crammed and jammed in everywhere, but there was nowhere near enough room for it all.

The kitchen is large, but the wood stove needs a good blacking. I expect that will be one of my first tasks as soon as we are more settled. There is a long, wooden table with stools around it and a sink with no sign of spigots for running water. When I had a chance to explore a bit, I discovered some outbuildings in back and a shed for a horse. James's room is back there as well. I do not think he is happy with that!

Worst of all, I think, is the smell. The air is ripe with it. The same smell of smoke as struck us at the station, but added to that, the house stinks of dirty drains and heaven only knows what else. The first morning we were here I got a fire going in the stove and unpacked some pots and dishes and managed to make a soup, but Missus Bradley was having none of it. She stayed in bed with a headache for most of the day.

Not a very good beginning.

Friday, May 18th, 1866

You would think that things could not get worse. You would be wrong.

Monday, May 21st, 1866

I am so tired. We are still unpacking and trying to arrange the furniture in some kind of order and I am kept hopping to the nearby shops to buy supplies. A brief respite yesterday because it was the sabbath. Mister and Missus Bradley are Church of England but, to Missus Bradley's dismay, when we arrived she found that the only church of that persuasion is away over on the other side of the city, so here they are holding services in the courthouse, of all places. Missus Bradley was certain she could see prisoners looking down at them through their barred windows. She was most upset about it.

I was allowed to attend Mass at St. Joseph's. I was overcome by the number of very fine people there, but I kept to the back and made myself small. No one noticed me.

Missus Bradley is beyond unhappy with this situation. I overheard Mister Bradley trying to comfort her, and saying that they are just renting this house, and promising that he would build her a fine house as soon as they were confident that the capital of the Province of Canada would not be moved again. It has moved so often, but usually between Québec City and Toronto — both civilized towns. I don't think anyone is happy about this, but of course we must obey the Queen.

I have just been able to catch glimpses of the Parliament Buildings up on the hill, built here to house the government of the United Province of Canada. The buildings are said to be magnificent. Miss Edwards told me all about them and I cannot wait to see them up close, but all is at sixes and sevens here and I fear it will be a long while before I get a day off for my own pleasure.

I cannot help thinking about Mary Margaret, who is at home and happy with her Donny and her wedding plans, while I am here in this miserable town, so far away.

It is not fair!

Wednesday, May 23ʳᵈ, 1866

Order is beginning to be established, but there is still much too much to fit into this house. Missus Bradley and I have worked from dawn to dusk trying to get everything organized. At least she is coping better with things, and I think is beginning to get used to me, but I am afraid all is not well between her and Mister Bradley. He is off to his duties in Parliament every day and she is getting fair knackered. She was very short with him when he came home late last evening and he was in a temper. I am not a very good cook and I had burned most of the dinner at noon. That did not help matters at all. Missus Bradley hardly touched the food and, even though she tried to hide it, she sicked most of it up afterwards.

She is not a very strong person to begin with, though, and I am beginning to suspect she might be in the family way. I hope it was that, and not my miserable cooking.

I was right to worry about the lack of spigots. There is no running water in the house. We're to buy barrels of water for fifteen cents a gallon off a delivery cart that comes round to the door. There are only primitive wooden drains for the water, and no facilities for sewage at all. I have to empty the chamber pots every morning and that is a disgusting job. For myself and any other servants we might get, there is a smelly outhouse in the back.

There is no garbage collection, so the contents of the chamber pots and the scraps from the kitchen are just tossed into a pile at the back of the house, as close to the bushes as I can get. It seems that the pile of refuse is collected once every spring. I surely hope that they haven't already done the collection for this year.

My own family's little house in Québec City might have been humble, but even it was far better than this!

Friday, May 25th, 1866

We have a cook! I don't know who is more relieved, Mister and Missus Bradley or myself.

Monday, May 28th, 1866

Missus Ramsay, the cook, started today. Dinner at noon was a delight, as was supper this evening. She has a small room in the garret. She is a rather stern person, given to ordering me around. I am none too happy with that, but fear there is nothing to do but hop to her wishes.

First off she was at me for not having cleaned the wood stove up and blacked it, but, truth to tell, I have not had a moment. Then, when I started to explain, she just cut me off and told me to get to it. No sooner had I started than Missus Bradley rang to ask me to help her unpack another trunk. Then it was time to walk the infernal dog. I cannot say that I walk him. He walks me. Drags me, more like. Brutus has done nothing to change my opinion of dogs.

Wednesday, May 30th, 1866

Well, the wretched stove is blacked and as clean as I could get it, which was none too clean. Satisfied Cook, though, thanks be.

The man who brings our water is nice, but his son, who helps him, is a very cheeky boy. Brian the boy's name is. He told me that straight off, adding that his friends call him Briney. As I have no intention of being one of his friends, I shall call him Brian. When I call him anything at all, that is. Which may not be often. He asked me what my name was and when I told him it was Rosie, he said his mam had a cow named Rosie!

Thursday, May 31st, 1866

We have bought a cow too, for fresh milk and butter. She is not named Rosie. She is called Daisy. Actually, she is a pleasant enough beast, but rather stupid, in the way of cows. She cost forty dollars! She is established in the shed next to the pony trap and the master's horse, but she is allowed out in the back garden during the day as it is well fenced. Cook is asking for chickens. She is marking out a site for a kitchen garden and I will help her dig it and plant vegetables. Peas, corn, beans and tomatoes to start with.

There is another lad who brings wood for the woodpile. He is a French boy and his name is Jean-Louis. He is much more polite than that Brian boy.

We must keep the pile stocked so that we have enough for the stove, and in the winter we will need it for the fires, but it seems there might be a problem with that. Mister Bradley reads from the newspaper, the *Citizen*, of an evening, and sometimes I am able to listen. I like that, as with the door open between the parlour and the kitchen, I overhear all manner of interesting things.

One evening he was reading a letter complaining about logs continually being stolen from woodpiles. The writer suggested making an auger hole in logs and plugging them with gunpowder. I expect that they would explode when someone took an axe to them to split the wood. It seemed a rather drastic solution to me and to Missus Bradley as well, but I heard Cook snort an agreement with the idea. It would go very badly with any thief who tried to steal our wood, I think.

Friday, June 1ˢᵗ, 1866

Mister Bradley looked very grim this evening at supper. Seems there's something dreadful serious brewing, but he would not speak of it.

Monday, June 4ᵗʰ, 1866

It was something serious indeed! The Province of Canada has been invaded! That Brian boy told me this morning when he delivered the water. He was all excited and had armed himself with a stick. I do believe he expected to see American soldiers marching down the street at any moment. He is most certainly a foolish boy.

Still, it was worrisome and I'm all in a muddle as to what happened, but here is what I was able to make out from what the master told the missus today at noontime. No one seemed to notice me hanging at the door, so I listened for all I was worth. Da has always been mad keen about politics and I think it has worn off on me.

It seems there is a group of Irishmen in the United States of America who are determined to make Ireland independent of Britain. No news there, of course, but what was surprising is that these people, Fenians they call themselves, have got a stronghold in America and they've decided to establish a base here in the Province of Canada. I cannot for the life of me figure out what they mean to gain by that. Nevertheless, they crossed over near a town called Niagara this Saturday past and there was a battle at a place called Ridgeway near there. Seems the fighting lasted for either thirty minutes or three hours — Mister Bradley heard both — but it was fierce and there were many killed and wounded. Mister Bradley said for a while it looked as if the Fenians would win, but finally they withdrew back across the Niagara River to Buffalo.

Missus Bradley was in a right state. Mister Bradley was quick to reassure her that the battle was far from here and we were never in any danger.

"But it's not just the Irish," Missus Bradley insisted. "There's talk that since the North has won the war between the states in America, and the slaves have been set free, the Americans might be considering invading us next."

That worried me. My da told me tales of the war in 1812 when the United States invaded the Canadian colonies with the excuse of liberating us from the English. We'd sent them packing then. Surely we could do it again, but I didn't particularly want to put it to the test.

Mister Bradley's next words reassured me somewhat. "In that case, making this godforsaken town the capital might just have been a good idea," he said. "Any invading soldiers would get lost looking for the place."

Later

In spite of Mister Bradley's reassuring words this morning, when he came home from Parliament this evening, I overheard him grumbling that all civil servants must take part in military drills from now on. Just in case. He is even going to be wearing a uniform!

He did not seem too pleased about that, and it only frightened Missus Bradley all the more.

Tuesday, June 5th, 1866

What with the worry of it all, Missus Bradley has taken to her bed. I am run off my feet fetching and carrying for her, and doing Cook's bidding, and walking that wretched dog, and I don't know what else. At least by the time I have a moment to myself at bedtime I am too tired to feel lonely. At most I can just scribble a few lines here. I fear Ottawa is going to be the death of me.

And I lie. Tired or not, I do feel lonely. I feel lonely at bedtime, I feel lonely when I wake in the morning, and I feel lonely every blessed moment of the day. I wonder is Mary Margaret wed yet. I wonder how the little ones are. I wonder if they miss me. I wonder if Mam and Da miss me.

There. I've made a huge blot right in the middle of the page with my foolish weeping. Sure it does no good at all. If I think my lot is hard, I should remember what the lives of those slaves in America were like before the war set them free. They were sold away from their families, not just moved away, and in many cases they never saw the people they loved again. They couldn't even write to them — Da told me they were punished with whipping and even death if they so much as learned to read, let alone write.

I'll send Mam and Da a long letter now and stop feeling so sorry for myself.

Wednesday, June 6th, 1866

They had the official opening of the new Parliament Buildings today. Mister Bradley wanted Missus Bradley to go with him for the ceremony, but she didn't feel up to it. He seemed disappointed, but told her all about it when he got back this evening. Me listening at the door as usual, and I begin to understand a bit more about what this Confederation means.

He said that Mister John A. Macdonald made a fine speech, as did Mister George-Étienne Cartier. Those two gentlemen, who lead the Conservative Party, along with Mister George Brown, who leads the Reform Party, formed the coalition that governs our province now. They are all keen supporters of the cause of the Confederation of the Province of Canada with the other British provinces. It took me a bit of thinking to piece it together, for Cook kept asking for help with the cleaning up and I didn't hear all that Mister Bradley said, but it seems that if Confederation happened, we would be a country of our own, even though we would still be part of the British Empire. It's all a bit confusing, but I know something about it already because Da was always on about it. It was Da who explained the coalition when it happened two years ago. Seems like the two parties could never agree on anything, and with the threat of American invasion, something had to be done, so they all joined together. Da explained it as being like what children will do when they're up against someone bigger — stick together. Sounded like a good solution to me.

Mister

Later

Oh, what a narrow squeak I've just had!

Cook nosed into my tiny room without warning while I was writing this, to give me some orders for tomorrow. I barely had time to tuck my journal under my quilt. If she had seen it I know she would have demanded to see what I was writing, and I would never want her to read my words about her and about Mister and Missus Bradley! I doubt that I would be whipped, like the poor unfortunate slaves, but she would have me out on my ear, I'm sure of it.

She did, however, see all today's newspapers spread out here on my bed. Didn't she just rip into me! I am supposed to take them out in the evening after Mister Bradley is done with them and tear them up to be used in the outhouse and as fire starters, but I carry them to my room first and read as much as I can. I want to know what is going to happen to my country — I pretend I might be having a conversation with Da about it. I had to bundle them up and dispose of them quickly after she came tonight, though, and I am still smarting from the dressing down she gave me. It is really not good to be on the rough side of her tongue.

I will just finish up quickly now and then hide this away under my pillow.

What I was about to say was that Mister Cartier is French. I have a few words of French, but I found out how to spell his name from the papers.

Mister Bradley also talked about another man, Mister Thomas D'Arcy McGee. He's Irish and very loud and noisy on the subject of Confederation, according to Mister Bradley. It didn't sound as if Mister Bradley totally approved of him, even though he is such a great supporter of the cause. I heard Mister Bradley say that some people even suspected Mister McGee of somehow being behind the Fenian raid into New Brunswick last April. When Missus

Bradley asked him why Mister McGee would do that, Mister Bradley said those same people thought he might be trying to throw a scare into the people of the Maritimes and turn their opinion in favour of Confederation, but Mister Bradley didn't believe it for a moment.

"There is a good deal of opposition out there in the Maritimes to joining this Confederation of the provinces into one country," he said, "and McGee is certainly a wild man, but he wouldn't go that far."

Mister Bradley also does not entirely approve of something Mister Macdonald does — the way he dresses. It sounds very peculiar. It seems he doesn't dress in the usual dark-coloured clothes that most men wear. Instead, he wears a combination of checkered jackets and trousers and neckerchiefs that Mister Bradley said are most unsuitable.

I am thinking how much more elegant Mister Bradley must look in his black frock coat. I rub the collar down with Fuller's Earth every morning to remove the macassar oil he uses to keep his hair tidy, and I take care to sponge any spots off very carefully. He is a very elegant dresser, is Mister Bradley.

I am not quite so scared of him as I was. He is kind to Missus Bradley. Spoils her, though, I fear. Sometimes she seems a right child. When he talks about his work in government of an evening she never pays much attention.

Thursday, June 7th, 1866

Missus Bradley puked non-stop nearly all day and cannot keep even a sip of soup down. Cook is frantic.

A babe is on the way for sure.

Friday, June 8th, 1866

It seems like it's not only in the Maritimes that there's opposition to Confederation. Mister Bradley came home tonight in a fair temper. Seems a Mister Antoine-Aimé Dorion is stirring people up against it in what used to be Canada East before Canada East and Canada West joined together to become the Province of Canada. Canada East is mostly French — despite a number of families like mine who live there — and Mister Dorion is afraid that Confederation would mean that French Canadians would be outnumbered in the new country. But it has taken a long time and a lot of work to get this close to Confederation, Mister Bradley said, and he is impatient with anyone who still puts objections in the way of it. He says he cannot understand why everyone is not in favour of our becoming a country. He should talk to Da. Da always said that you could never get everyone to have the same opinion about anything.

I wonder what would happen if Canada East did decide not to join in. Would that mean that my family would be living in a separate country? That's a worrisome thought.

By coincidence, when I was ripping up today's newspapers — and reading them, of course — I came across an article that talked about this very problem. It quoted Mister Cartier as saying that French Canadians need not worry, as they would be able to keep their own culture and language. Then the article went on to warn the people of Canada East that if they didn't join, the new United States might just take them over. What in the world would happen to my family then? How I wish I could talk to Da about it and hear what he thinks. Maybe he could reassure me.

Saturday, June 9th, 1866

There's no getting away from that Brian boy. He talks non-stop when he delivers the water and doesn't even seem to notice that I am not answering him. This morning he tracked mud into the kitchen. James was standing by and, although it was really no business of his, he saw fit to give the boy the rough side of his tongue in his usual unpleasant way. The boy is a nuisance, no doubt about it, but I found myself getting angry and even defending him a little bit. James is so unpleasant, I have lost all fear of him and dislike him intensely.

Monday, June 11th, 1866

Cook taught me how to milk Daisy today. I am not very good at it yet, but I prayed to Saint Bridget to help me learn. She is the saint of all things to do with the dairy, so if anyone can help me it will be her. Cook does not have much patience and Daisy doesn't take kindly to my efforts. If that cow is not switching me with her tail she is stamping her hoof at me. I don't think she would kick me, but she might.

We also dug out a small corn patch and planted rhubarb slips near the back kitchen door. Tomorrow we will dig another patch for potatoes.

I am fair exhausted.

Wednesday, June 13th, 1866

Added beets and turnips to the garden. It's a bit late to be planting them, but we can't help that. I dislike turnips immensely. Brutus trampled the rhubarb slips and we had to replant them. I hope he tramples the turnips when they come up.

Friday, June 15th, 1866

Mister Bradley came home this evening wearing his uniform! He looks very fine in it, but he hates it. He complains that it is heavy and itches.

Nevertheless, he invited Missus Bradley to walk up to Parliament Hill to watch him drill with his unit on Tuesday. To my surprise, as she seems to be feeling a mite better, she agreed. She is to go next week and she wishes me to accompany her, as Mister Bradley will not be able to bring her back, and she does not wish to walk home alone.

At last I will get away from this wretched house and see the Parliament Buildings up close!

Sunday, June 17th, 1866

When the family came home from their church service today, I heard Missus Bradley talking about the collection that had been raised for their new church. Mister Bradley was impressed because that outrageous Mister D'Arcy McGee had contributed, even though he is a Catholic. I wonder why he would do that. He must be a very open-minded gentleman.

Tuesday, June 19th, 1866

Finally! A lovely day indeed. After breakfast Missus Bradley told me to make myself ready and we would be going up to the Parliament Buildings. This house we are renting is in a part of Ottawa called Upper Town, and the buildings are near to us, up on the river.

It was a bright day, and hot. I put on my best dress — the one that used to be Mary Margaret's — and wore a shawl, but the sun was so warm I didn't really need it. Then I helped Missus Bradley dress. She seemed in much better spirits. It took us less than half an hour to walk up Elgin Street to Parliament Hill. Mister Bradley escorted us, and it was just as well that he did. There were military units marching, bugles and fifes and drums playing — soldiers everywhere. Mister Bradley might be certain the invaders could never find us away up here, but the city looks like it's prepared for war! For a few moments, he looked as if he was about to change his mind and take us back home, but Missus Bradley was having none of that. "We've come this far, I'm not going back without seeing the Parliament Buildings up close, and watching you drill," she said. I was surprised at how determined she was.

Mister Bradley gave in — he always gives in to her — and walked us up to the buildings. He made certain we were in a safe place and well positioned to see everything, then he left us to join his regiment.

I was not prepared for the buildings being so beautiful. And they are so big! They fair shone in the sun, sort of a deep golden colour, with glistening grey slate roofs with patterns etched into them in green. There was ironwork all around the edges, painted blue and gold. Most amusing for me were all the carved stone faces looking down on the people below. Truly, the whole effect was magical.

There was a crowd gathered there too, waiting for the Civil Service Militia to do their drill. Our places were right at the front. How grand when they marched out, almost all in step. We picked out Mister Bradley and I was very proud to see that he was one of the tallest and, I thought, one of the most distinguished of the marchers. They kept their eyes straight front, but I swear I saw him peek out of the corner of one eye to see Missus Bradley, then his face lit up and he broke out in a small smile, in spite of the horrible uniform.

We walked around for a bit after the drill was over. I was afraid Missus Bradley would tire, but she did not. The buildings are not finished yet around the back, but there was a path that ran around the top of the bluff right along the river's edge. It was a little rough, but pretty, so we followed it, the pair of us entranced with the view. We could see green, forested hills rising on the other side.

Missus Bradley was in a better humour today and seemed happy to talk to me more than she has so far, and I felt a bit more at ease with her. She told me that across the river is where my family's part of the country — the part that used to be Canada East — begins. Staring across the river and thinking about how very far away my home was over there made me so homesick!

And now I'm making myself sad again just writing about it.

Enough! On with my story.

By the time we retraced our steps and began to make our way back home, the crowd had grown and we were forced almost to push our way through it. The wooden sidewalks on Sparks

Street are narrow and, before we realized what was happening, a group of rowdy boys pushed past us and forced Missus Bradley off the walk and into the mud. I grabbed for her, but couldn't reach her arm. She would have fallen if another boy hadn't darted forward and caught her. And who was it but himself, that annoying Brian.

I suppose I shouldn't call him annoying now, because he certainly saved her from a bad fall and kept us company all the way home. That was fortunate too, because, wouldn't you know it, when we reached our street, what did we find but two disgusting hogs rooting in the mud right in front of our house!

"Shoo them off, Rosie," Missus Bradley said. "I am going to go in and ask Cook to put the kettle on for tea." She was looking a little pale and I think was still upset about the near fall.

Shoo them off, indeed. Plain to see she had never tried to shoo off a pig. I ran at them, shouting, and each one headed off in a different direction. If Briney hadn't been there I never would have gotten them sorted out. By the time we got them off down the street, I was hot and bothered and in a right mess, and my best dress was muddy again, but when I looked at Briney I couldn't help laughing. He had done the greater part of the chasing and he was mud from top to toe. I thought he might be fashed at my laughing, but he just joined in.

"Sure, I don't know why you're laughing," he said. "You're as dirty as I am, Rosie Dunn."

Before I could answer that, Missus Bradley came out with a bundle.

"Your father tells me you have older sisters at home, Brian," she said. "Perhaps they could use these dresses that I can't wear anymore."

That was thoughtful of her and for once Briney was speechless. He just tipped his hat and stuttered something no one could understand. Missus Bradley laughed and handed him the bundle, then he was off.

I wish she had thought to ask me if I wanted one of those dresses, but I suppose she thought they would not be suitable for someone my age. Still, if I can wear Mary Margaret's cast-offs, I could have worn one of hers.

I just realized I called him Briney. Oh well. It does seem to suit him better than plain Brian.

Wednesday, June 20th, 1866

Briney came around with the water today. He started in on his teasing, but somehow I didn't seem to mind it as much. I don't think he means anything by it. It's just his way. In fact, he has further endeared himself to Missus Bradley. The backyard is fenced in, but the front is not, so he offered to build a fence around it to protect it from pigs. He told her his sisters were over the moon with the dresses.

Cook is not so taken with him, though. He made a mess in the kitchen again. When he carried one of the barrels of water in, it sprang a leak and dripped all over the floor.

It wasn't his fault, but she was on at him in a fierce way and made him take it back, still dripping, and give us another, all for the same price. Then she made him clean up the mess. I felt sorry for the hapless boy and helped.

Friday, June 22nd, 1866

Mister and Missus Bradley entertained last evening. A group of friends came over to play cards. Mam doesn't approve of card playing and I have never seen the games played before. I was so intrigued, I bumped into Mister Bradley's chair and almost dropped a plate of cake on the floor. He raised an eyebrow at my clumsiness, but fortunately didn't say anything. I was embarrassed, though, and kept my wits about me for the rest of the evening. Mister D'Arcy McGee was amongst the guests and he was very loud and boisterous, just as Mister Bradley described him. I was eager to see him and I was not disappointed. Faith, I could hardly take my eyes off him. I kept sneaking peeks at him around the doorframe from the kitchen when no one was watching me.

There was a spot of bother, though, that threatened to spoil the evening for a moment. One of

Mister Bradley's guests began to talk very loudly about what he called "this Confederation nonsense." He said he could see no sense in it, and couldn't understand why people couldn't just leave things the way they were.

Mister McGee got very red in the face and looked as if he were going to explode. Before he could say anything, though, Missus Bradley cut in and suggested a new game for them to play, and the confrontation was avoided.

But that means it's not just some of the French in Canada East who oppose Confederation. There are English people here in Ottawa too. That makes me even more worried. Before I came here I had no idea how important this whole business was, and how it might affect me and my family.

I'm beginning to think that it might be best if they would just forget the whole idea and get on with things as they are, but I suppose that's just me thinking selfishly.

Missus Bradley slept in this morning. I expect she was tired, but she enjoyed the evening so much, it was surely worth it. Cook sent me up with a light breakfast for her at around 10 o'clock, and she seemed restored and in very good humour.

Monday, June 25th, 1866

Mister Bradley agreed to pay for the wood for the fence, so Briney turned up with Jean-Louis today. They brought a load of lumber in his wagon and set to work. They are hammering away as I write. It is very hot today. I think I will take them a cup of water.

Later

That Jean-Louis is very shy. Perhaps it's because he doesn't speak much English. He actually blushed bright red when I gave him his cup of water and couldn't look me in the eye. I think he is sweet. He's certainly not the brash lad that Briney is.

It's amusing to watch them work together. Briney doesn't speak French, so they seem to communicate mostly by waving their hands around at each other. It works, though, as the fence is coming along apace. Mister Bradley says the French and the Irish often do not get on very well here in Ottawa and fights break out constantly, but Briney and Jean-Louis seem to be friendly enough.

Wednesday, June 27th, 1866

The fence is done. Missus Bradley is right pleased with it. She gave the boys each fifteen cents for their work and sent Cook out to them with some cool lemonade. That fence will be a blessing. It's not just pigs that roam the streets, but cows are driven by our house almost every day and they seem to love to take side trips into our front garden. I think Daisy calls them. Perhaps she wants the company. This evening one cow stopped on her way and rested her head on the fence and looked quite longingly at the garden that is now out of her reach. Daisy bellowed from the back, but to no avail. She will have to get used to being lonely. Perhaps it will make her more co-operative when I milk her. Yesterday she kicked the pail over when it was half full. Cook was fair riled. I heard her praying to Saint Bridget too. I hope it works, but that cow has a mind of her own, she does.

Friday, June 29th, 1866

The heat is dreadful. Missus Bradley is doing poorly again.

Briney wants to show me the sawmill across the river. His older brother works there. I wasn't that eager to go, but he assures me that it's something to see. The logs come down from the forest upriver in great rafts — so big they are that men build shanties on them and live on them for the journey down to the mills here in Ottawa and farther downriver in Montreal and Québec City. He made it all sound so interesting that I found myself agreeing to go with him on my first free day.

It wasn't until after he left that I realized I have no notion at all of when or even if I get a free day. I certainly haven't so far and I don't dare ask about it.

Monday, July 2nd, 1866

The problem solved itself. Missus Bradley spoke to me yesterday when I got back from Mass and asked me if I wanted a day to myself.

"You've earned it, Rosie," she said. "You're a good worker."

Then she frowned a bit and asked me if I knew what I wanted to do on my day off. She wasn't certain that I should be traipsing around on my own in the city. I had to bite my lip to keep from laughing. Sure, I've been "traipsing around" the city of Québec by myself since I was ten years old.

I assured her that I wouldn't be on my own, that Briney had offered to show me around. But that didn't seem to reassure her very much and she hemmed and hawed a bit about how it might not be suitable for a young girl to be out on her own with a boy.

I think the rules for people such as the Bradleys are very different from those for us common folk. Very glad I am to be one of the common folk. I think we have more fun. I know my mam was always keen for us young ones to learn to take care of ourselves as soon as we could.

Then I wondered how I would let Briney know. I needn't have worried. He came around this morning, even though it wasn't the regular day for water delivery, and we agreed to set out after I had helped Cook with the breakfast. Missus Bradley could not eat much, but Mister Bradley tucked into his usual porridge, ham and eggs and hotcakes very handily. I must admit I was impatient to see him finish and perhaps I cleared the dishes away a mite too quickly, as he was left holding the last bite of hotcakes on his fork when I whisked his plate away. He raised an eyebrow, but thanks be didn't say anything. Cook did, though. She gave me a tongue-lashing in the kitchen that lasted the whole time we were cleaning up.

The very minute we were through, I was out the door to find Briney waiting for me, but before we could set off, Missus Bradley buttonholed Briney and gave him a stern talking-to as to how he should take care of me and make certain that we didn't get into any trouble.

I think he was a mite flabbergasted, but he responded politely and gave her earnest assurances that he would care for me as if I were one of his own sisters, and then we were off.

We walked along the canal to the river and stopped to watch the boats locking through. I hadn't seen that yet. There are a series of something like pens in the canal, called locks, and huge gates that close them off from each other. Boats sail into the first lock from the canal, then a man turns a big wheel up on top of the gates behind the boats and those gates close, shutting them into the lock. Then, somehow or other, they start letting the water out.

I think they can open little gates at the bottom of the big ones, until the water in that lock is down level with the water in the next lock. Then the man opens the gates in front of the boats by turning the wheel on the top of those gates, and the boats make their way out into that next lock. He closes the gates behind them once more, and lets the water out of the lock, then he opens the gates in front of them to let the boats go out yet again into the next lock.

There are eight of these locks that the boats have to go through until, finally, they are down at the level of the river and they sail out into it. Briney says they just reverse the procedure and fill each lock back up when boats want to go from the river up to the canal. I wanted to wait and watch that, but Briney was keen to get on to the sawmill and show me the rafts.

We walked along the riverbank up to the rapids at the Chaudière Falls. The sawmill was opposite us on the other bank. I could see huge piles of sawdust burning, and when the wind shifted toward us it was all I could do to breathe. The smoke was so thick it set me to coughing. That's where the horrible stench of smoke in the town comes from. I was just about to tell Briney I couldn't take another minute of it when he grabbed my arm and shouted, "Look there, Rosie! There comes a raft down the slider!"

I looked, and saw the most enormous raft hurtling down the river toward the falls. I was certain it would go over and be dashed to pieces, but the men standing on it guided it to a spot over beside the falls, where it was diverted away from the main part of the river.

"There's a slider there," Briney told me. "It's a place where they clear the rocks away and build a wood ramp, and the rafts just slide down it and avoid the falls completely."

As the raft swept back into the river below the falls and on down, I could see the shacks, the ones that Briney had told me about, set up on it. There was even smoke coming up from a cook fire on one of them. It was such an amazing sight that I decided I could put up with the smoke. We watched for an hour, but didn't see another raft go by. We did see smaller ones brought up against the shore to the sawmill, though. I expect those would be the ones that the mill would cut into lumber.

That mill has certainly made a mess of the river. Sawdust and wood shavings and all manner of disgusting stuff was piled in the water around it. Almost choked the river up, it did.

Finally, it was time to come back. I'm in my nook behind the kitchen now, writing while everyone else has gone to bed.

It was an exciting day, but now the loneliness has set in again. Evenings are the hardest. I wonder if I am missed as much at home as I miss all of them. My head tells me that of course I am, but my heart worries that I will be forgotten. I hope Mary Margaret realizes what a sacrifice I have made for her.

Wednesday, July 4th, 1866

A letter from home! It arrived this afternoon and I tucked it into my pocket to read tonight in the privacy of my own room. I was afraid to read it in front of Cook because I thought I might weep, and weep I did. Floods. Mam wrote that they are all well, although the little ones have all had colds. I worried for Bridget at that, but Mam said she was fine. The big news, of course, is that Mary Margaret is wed. I am happy for her, in spite of everything. I held the letter to my nose and I swear I could smell all the good smells of home in it. I've never been so happy and so sad all at once in my life.

I will stop now and write back to them. Missus Bradley gave me paper and an envelope and said that Mister Bradley would mail my response tomorrow. She asked if Mary Margaret was wed yet and I told her she was. She frowned and sniffed a bit at that, but then said she would drop a little something in the mail for Mary Margaret as a wedding gift, so perhaps she has forgiven her.

Friday, July 6th, 1866

Cook made a new dish with the eggs this morning. They were all stirred up in the pan. She called it "scrambled eggs." Mister Bradley was very dubious about trying them. Said they looked too messy, but then he tried them, and ate every scrap, so I suppose he liked them.

Wednesday, July 11th, 1866

So busy! I haven't had a moment to write in my journal. I just fall into bed exhausted at night. Cook has had me digging and weeding the garden without stop. The weather has been hot. Good for growing, and our vegetables are doing well, but there has not been much rain. We collect what little there is in a rain barrel, and I must water the young plants daily or they will die. It is very satisfying to see them grow bigger and taller every day. Faith, I think sometimes they are even taller in the evening than in the morn.

It annoys me intensely to see James lounging about watching us work away in this heat. He, of course, would not deign to dirty his hands, and he turns up his nose quite obviously at me. He takes good care not to look down on Cook, though. That would be the end of good meals for him if he did. Unfortunately, I am so unimportant in this house that he can snub me as much as he wishes. Oh, how I dislike him!

I wonder if my letter has reached home yet.

Friday, July 13th, 1866

Missus Bradley is feeling the heat very badly. Cook tries to make light soups for her, but she cannot seem to eat. To make matters worse, because the weather has been so dry there have been a lot of forest fires across the river and now even more smoke hangs like a pall over the city. The mills themselves keep up such a screeching and hammering that it is enough to drive a body mad.

How could a town be more horrid than this one? Whatever was Queen Victoria thinking when she chose it to be the capital?

Monday, July 16th, 1866

The heat continues. This morning Missus Bradley told me to take the afternoon off and go somewhere cool. There is nowhere cool to go, but Briney came by with the water and asked me to go blueberry picking with him. I was more than happy to do so.

We left straightaway after dinner at noon and crossed the river over to the hills on the other side. There was a profusion of blueberries growing all around the stony hillsides, and even though the mosquitoes were bothersome, we picked until all the buckets we had brought with us were filled. Cook says we will make flummery with the berries.

Tuesday, July 17th, 1866

Cook taught me how to make blueberry flummery. It was delicious. I have never tasted it before. This is the recipe:

> Stew 3 pints of blueberries with 1 of
> sugar. When the berries have been
> stewing for about 15 minutes, stir in
> a teacupful of flour, and stir the whole
> time until it becomes thick.

We let it cool and then ate it with cream. Missus Bradley even managed to eat some and it seemed to make her feel better. Cook was disappointed because she wanted to add a bit of lemon juice and peel to it, but there are no lemons to be had in Ottawa.

I hope Briney comes by tomorrow, as I've saved him some.

The heat is really unbearable. It was actually over 85 degrees today and not a breath of a breeze. Missus Bradley is suffering.

Wednesday, July 18th, 1866

Great news! Mister Bradley came home this evening to tell us that he is sending Missus Bradley to Cacouna for the summer, and I am to go too. Cacouna is a town on the south shore of the St. Lawrence River, away down past Québec City. He is worried that the heat is distressing to Missus Bradley. It seems that many of the other families go there in the summer to get away from the heat here. The town is right on the river and is much cooler with the breezes off the water. Mister Bradley has arranged for us to stay at a hotel and we leave next week on a steamer.

He will have to return to Ottawa after he gets us settled, as plans for Confederation are going ahead apace and he is needed here. Mister Macdonald, Mister Cartier, Mister Brown and a delegation of other men are planning to go to England in November to work out all the details and, although he will not be among them, Mister Bradley will have to work on the preparations for the trip. He'll return to fetch us home, however.

It will be grand, but the whole house is in turmoil, packing and getting ready to go.

I'm to travel on a steamship and stay in a hotel. Fancy that! I can't help feeling a little smug that I am to enjoy this instead of Mary Margaret. Not a very noble thought, but there, I have to have some consolation, don't I?

Sunday, July 22nd, 1866

Now I am in trouble. I got home from Mass before the Bradleys returned from their church and Cook was just taking the roast of beef out of the oven. She put it on the kitchen table and told me to make the gravy while she went up to her room for a clean apron. I thought I would just nip out to the garden to pick a tomato and some early peas before I started on the gravy. While I was out there, I saw Brutus tear out of the kitchen door with something in his mouth, and disappear back around Daisy's shack. I didn't think much of it — the beast is always tearing around and getting in the way. If anything, I was just grateful that he was out of the house. That's when I heard Cook screech. I ran back in and she was standing staring at the table in a right state. Staring at an empty platter with but a smear of meat juice on it. That wretched dog had stolen the whole joint and I am to blame for it.

What a to-do when the family returned and there was nothing but soup for their Sunday dinner. I am in disgrace. That beast will be the death of me. And of course James had to give me a good glare too. He obviously dislikes me as much as I do him, but I can't for the life of me understand why. What have I ever done to him? Perhaps he just thinks himself much more grand than any lowly servant girl.

They're still taking me to Cacouna, though. And thanks be, Cook and the dog are both staying here, and James will be returning with Mister Bradley.

Monday, July 23rd, 1866

We're off tomorrow morning early. The house is all at sixes and sevens. Must run. Missus Bradley is calling for me to help with the packing.

Tuesday, July 24th, 1866

I'm on the boat! We boarded early this morning. There was such a hustle and bustle on the docks,

Missus Bradley and I were fair confused, but Mister Bradley soon had it all sorted out. I was sent to find my berth below decks and that's where I am now. I have a cosy bunk in the women's section. There is such a to-ing and fro-ing that no one is paying any attention to me at all, so I have pulled out my journal to make this quick note.

The boat's whistle just let out a tremendous blast. We must be sailing. I'm off to the deck to watch us leave.

Later

Oh, it was fine watching the boat leave the dock. The great paddlewheels on the sides churn up the water no end and black smoke just poured out of the funnel. The river is choppy and I'm finding it hard to move around. Even harder to write. I'm making a right mess of this!

A cabin boy has just found me to tell me that my missus wants me up at her cabin to help her unpack. I'll tuck this away in my bundle and stow it under my mattress. *Stow* is a good nautical word. I heard a sailor use it.

Later again

We are well under way. That's another nautical term. The sailors almost speak a foreign language, it is so different. I'm tucked into my berth for the night and have a bit of time to write. A right large woman has the bunk next to mine, but she is not settled into it yet. Truth be told, I think she's making merry with some of the men. Someone's playing a fiddle and someone else is playing the harmonica and some people are dancing. It does sound lively.

Mister and Missus Bradley have a grand cabin up on the top deck next to the dining saloon. I helped Missus Bradley unpack, and then she wanted to lie down. I sat with her for a while. She was not well enough to go into the dining saloon for the noon meal, so I fetched her a bowl of soup. She was kind enough to have me fetch a bowl for myself as well, then she decided to rest and sent me away.

I spent the afternoon hanging over the rail and watching the water and the shore go by. The great paddlewheels on the sides make a thoroughly satisfying and peaceful *whoosh* with every turn. It is almost mesmerizing.

I have decided that travel by boat is infinitely better than travel by train. I spent a most delightful afternoon.

I saw a young girl around my age with another family, but I didn't have a chance to speak to her. She seemed to be a maidservant, as am I, and was helping her mistress to settle down onto a chair on the deck. I would have loved to speak to her. I wonder if by any chance she and that family are going to Cacouna as well.

The supper gong sounded at 6 o'clock and I

nipped back to see how Missus Bradley was faring. She was up and dressed and the colour was back in her cheeks. She told me she was going to play cards after supper and I was free to amuse myself for the rest of the evening.

The sailors brought down bowls of soup for us and loaves of bread and hard cheese. The fresh air must be giving me a great appetite because I was that hungry — it all tasted delicious.

We tied up for the night and after I ate I went up on deck again for a while. The moon was out and didn't it just look fine shining on the water. I drank the sight in. The breeze was gentle in my hair and I lifted my face to it, smelling all the good river smells. I could hear a brass and string band playing in the saloon. I hoped Missus Bradley was enjoying herself. Then I came back down here and curled up in my bunk to write this.

The dancing has stopped now. So has the fiddler. There is just the long, lonely sound of the harmonica. It's quite lovely, it is.

Whisht! Here comes my bunk mate. My, she does look large.

Friday, July 27th, 1866

The first chance I've had to write since we arrived in Cacouna. There is so much to tell, I don't know where to start. I suppose I should just start from where I left off on the boat.

I didn't sleep much that night. When Missus Tubbs — that's her name — arrived, she heaved herself up to the berth beside me and sort of exploded down with a huge sigh. She overflowed onto my bunk to such an extent that I squinched myself close to the hull of the ship, almost in terror that she would billow right over me and suffocate me. She was going to Montreal to visit her daughter. She has eight children, but this daughter is more trouble than all the rest put together, she said.

"A right baby she is," she said. "Never mind that she's wed and expecting a babe of her own. She'll never be able to get through it without me."

I wonder if that is the poor daughter's opinion too. Not much she'll have to say about it, I don't think.

That was only the first thing that I found out about her. It seemed that she was settled in to talking and she went on and on and on. I won't bother to put down all she said. Truth to tell, I kept dozing off, but when I did she gave me a good poke to startle me awake again, so I had to keep on making noises like I was listening. And, wouldn't you know it, she started in on Confederation. Seems it's all anybody is talking about these days. She couldn't see how it was going to do any good for the likes of her, she said. It wouldn't put more meat and potatoes on her table, and the whole business was just stirring the country up for no good reason. So there's someone else who doesn't agree with it.

I couldn't think of how to answer her, what with my own worries about it all, but as there was no chance of getting a word in anyway, it didn't really matter.

Then, just like that, between one word and another, she fell asleep. But then didn't she start in to snoring. Sounded like one of those great saws at the mill that Briney took me to. With hiccups. And snorts.

I was that sleepy the next morning. When I went up to help Missus Bradley, she caught me yawning and asked me if my sleeping arrangements had not been good. I told her it was not a problem. No sense worrying her. Besides, Missus Tubbs was getting off in Montreal and I wouldn't have to share sleeping quarters with her again.

As I went back out onto the deck I realized that something was about to happen. People crowded the railings and the sailors were hopping all about. Ahead of us the river was all in a turmoil. There were waves breaking from one side of the river to the other in all directions, it seemed. Some of them were huge.

I asked one of the sailors what it was. He said it was called the Lachine Rapids.

"Are we going to sail through them?" I asked. I couldn't believe it.

"That we are, Missy. Hang tight!"

Well, I decided that if we were going into that maelstrom, I was certainly going to have a good view of it. I dashed up to the bow of the boat. (That's the front. Another nautical term.)

I just reached the railing and with that we were into it. The boat steamed right into that wild water and within seconds we were being bounced around all over the place. I hung on for dear life. The ladies around me were screaming, and some of the gentlemen looked as if they were having a hard time not doing the same, but I just gloried in it. It was by far the most exciting thing that has ever happened to me and I didn't want to miss a moment of it. The spray from the waves we hit rose up almost to where I was standing.

Finally we sailed out and into the river proper. I had thought the river rough before, but after that it seemed as calm as a millpond.

What an adventure! I heard one of the ladies complaining later, saying that there was a perfectly good canal that we could have gone through and avoided the rapids altogether. A sailor told her that they go through them on purpose, to give the passengers some fun. She harrumphed mightily and declared that some people's idea of fun was not hers and she was most certainly going to complain to the captain.

I am so happy that we did it, though. I wouldn't have missed it for the world.

When Missus Tubbs got off in Montreal she enveloped me in those great soft arms and gave me a huge hug that stopped my breathing for several minutes. I couldn't help feeling a wee bit sorry for the daughter, but Missus Tubbs is a good soul and I suppose she means well.

One thing I did not know was that we would be docking in Québec City! When we got there, it was so hard to be so close to my family but not able to see them! With all the planning for this trip, it must not have occurred to the Bradleys that I would have wanted to. I suppose I can't blame them — they had a lot more on their minds than the wishes of an unimportant maidservant, but even though we weren't there for too long, I would have had time. I could see the monument erected to the memory of Wolfe and Montcalm and I knew that our house was not far behind it. What were Mam and Da doing right at that moment? What were the young ones doing? What would they have thought if they'd known I was so close?

I could hardly bear it when the boat started up again and we drew away from the pier.

When we arrived in Cacouna, watching the captain dock the boat was so breathtaking that it took my mind off my own misery somewhat. It was almost as exciting as going through the rapids. He came in at full speed to within about two boat lengths of the wharf, and then, just when I thought he was going to dash the boat right into the dock, he rang a bell to stop, whipped the wheel around to reverse, and laid the boat close alongside as neatly as a skiff coming in.

Mister Bradley and James saw to the unloading of all the baggage — enough to do us for a good year, I should think, although we'll only be here for a few weeks. Then we were taken by pony cart to the hotel where we will be staying. It's called Saint Lawrence Hall, and a very fine hotel it is. I even have my own room! Just a tiny dressing room off Missus Bradley's bedroom, but it is my own space and it is here that I am writing this in peace and comfort.

What I have seen of Cacouna looks delightful. There's a beach and there was a beautiful sunset over the river tonight. I never saw a lovelier sight. I can't wait to go exploring!

That is all that I can write tonight, though. Even though we have gas lamps here, I don't want to be using up too much. I wouldn't want to be scolded for it.

I wonder if the gas would run out if I kept it on for too long. Don't imagine so, as the lamps in the hotel seem to be on far into the night.

Monday, July 30ᵗʰ, 1866

It's like a holiday for me here, it is. And me who has never had a holiday in my life! I tend to Missus Bradley's needs in the morning and fetch and carry for her, but I don't have to do any of the cooking or cleaning. We go down to breakfast and Mister and Missus Bradley eat in the dining room, of course. James and I eat in the kitchen. I am not expected to work there, as the cook has two kitchen maids who help her, but I lend a hand whenever possible. James, of course, does not. He sits with the other manservants and is quite happy to be waited on. I ignore him. Mister Bradley will be leaving to go back to Ottawa soon and I will not have to deal with James after that.

Thursday, August 2nd, 1866

Mister Bradley and James have gone back to Ottawa and we have settled into a routine. After breakfast, if the day is fine, which it has been so far, we go down to the beach. This involves a lot of packing and carrying of chairs, sunshades, magazines, papers, hampers with foodstuffs and drinks, and I don't know what all. We are up above the river here and the beach is down below us, so everything has to be carted down a path and stairs that go down the riverbank to the beach below. We set everything up and are established there for the morning. I settle myself beside Missus Bradley and have a grand time watching the bathers and all the boats. Missus Bradley does not bathe, of course. She is beginning to show just a little. I do her laces up more and more loosely every day. I imagine when we go back to Ottawa she will have to confine herself to the house.

Oh, how I would love to bathe! But of course I have no bathing costume, so I content myself with hoisting up my skirts and paddling at the edge. How grand to feel the sand in between my bare toes. I was a little reluctant at first, and wouldn't go near the water. I felt I should stay with Missus Bradley, but she was having none of it. "Off you go," she said. "Enjoy yourself."

So enjoy myself I do.

I saw the girl who was on the boat with us. The family she works for sets up a little farther down the beach. She has a bathing costume and was right in the water, splashing with some children and having no end of a good time, by the looks of it. She's a pretty girl with masses of curls the colour of honey. I wonder if she's friendly. It would be nice to make a friend.

In the afternoons, Missus Bradley has her lie-down and I am free to roam around the town and explore to my heart's content. Missus Bradley doesn't seem to worry about me here.

I've found a general store nearby that's owned by a Monsieur Henri-Joseph Sirois. It is a fascinating place. It has all manner of spices and exotic-looking items. I summoned up the courage to ask and Monsieur Sirois was kind enough to show me the huge barrels his merchandise comes in, shipped by boats, called *goélettes*, from Québec City. Cook would be over the moon if she could shop there.

Even here the talk of Confederation goes on. It is the main subject on everyone's lips. I am amazed to hear some people argue vehemently against it. It sounds as if it will go through, though, like it or lump it.

Monday, August 6ᵗʰ, 1866

Church yesterday and then a day of rest and quiet. Missus Bradley goes to St. James the Apostle church, and I went to Mass at Saint Georges de Cacouna. A lovely little church it is. So peaceful and pretty.

Wednesday, August 8ᵗʰ, 1866

I met the girl I saw on the boat and on the beach! Her family is staying at another hotel, the Dufferin House, and there is a general store on the ground floor. Our hotel cook asked me if I would nip over and get some eggs there for her, and when I did I almost ran into that very girl. She is just as friendly as I had hoped, although perhaps a bit over-pleased with herself. Her name is Bessie and she was quick to tell me that the family she works for is one of the most important families in Ottawa. When I mentioned that the Bradleys live on King Street in Upper Town, her nose tilted just a trifle and she informed me very loftily that the family she works for lives on

Daly Street in the very fashionable district of Sandy Hill, just a block away from the fine stone house of the Queen's Printer, Monsieur George-Èdouard Desbarats. I know I've written that correctly, as she was quick to spell it out for me, although I must admit I had to bite my tongue to keep from telling her that I could spell names very well myself, thank you very much. I was the best speller in my class.

Besides, truth be told, I might not have been able to figure that one out.

We agreed to meet tomorrow afternoon. She has offered to lend me a bathing costume — she has two — and I will have a chance to bathe!

Thursday, August 9th, 1866

What a glorious day! Bessie lent me her bathing costume and I bathed in the river for ages this afternoon. At first I was very shy about appearing in public in such a scanty outfit — you could easily see my ankles — but all the other ladies and girls were doing it, and Missus Bradley insisted I try, so I took courage and plunged in. The water was cold, but the weather was sunny and hot, and it was grand. I like Bessie, even though she is bossy — everything must be done to her liking. Still, she is generous to a fault.

❧

Friday, August 10th, 1866

Now I'm fuming. I happened to mention something about Briney to Bossy Bessie this afternoon and her nose tilted up again in that annoying way that she has.

"Oh, that Irish boy who delivers your water," she said.

"Sure, you may not have noticed," I said to her with as much dignity as I could muster, letting my Irish speech come through a little thicker than usual, "'tis Irish I am too, and well proud of it."

At that she got all flustered and tight-lipped English and we parted on unfriendly terms.

Monday, August 13th, 1866

A lovely day today. I do believe this fresh air is doing Missus Bradley a world of good. She has colour in her cheeks and a bounce to her step. After breakfast she asked me if I would like to go for a walk with her, and of course I agreed. We set out in the bright sunshine, with a cool breeze coming off the river to keep us comfortable. We walked so far! I was worried that she would not be able to make it back to the hotel, but she insisted.

We went all the way to the Indian village that sits on the riverside where the land slopes more gradually to the water. It's a pretty village. There's one road that runs through the middle of it, with neat little cabins on either side. The road is little more than a grassy track, with a path running along one side of it. At the top we looked down to the wee houses with their red and blue-grey roofs. A rambling fence ran alongside the road to separate it from the fields surrounding the houses, but I didn't see any cattle. There were beaver and muskrat skins drying in some of the backyards, and some small kitchen gardens and patches of oats and wheat in the fields as well, but Missus Bradley told me the Indians — Maliseet, she said they were called — relied mostly on fishing and hunting for their food.

I was a mite concerned that we would not be welcome there, but that was pure foolishness. As soon as we got well into the village, a small horde of children surrounded us, chattering and laughing as they caught at our hands and tried to lead us to one cabin or another. Missus Bradley knew where to go, however, as our hotel keeper had given her the name of one particular woman. Missus Bradley asked for her and even though the children laughed at the way she pronounced the name, they led us to a cabin right at the river's edge.

A woman came out to greet us. I had expected that she would be in buckskins, but she was clothed in an ordinary blouse and long skirt. She was right welcoming and invited us to sit in the sun by her door. She brought out tea for both of us, then she brought out baskets that she had made out of split ash and sweet grass. They smelled so wonderful! Missus Bradley bought a lovely big one, then, to my surprise, she turned to me and said, "Pick one out for yourself, Rosie. Something to keep your treasures in."

Well, I don't have that many treasures, but there was one little box that this journal would fit in perfectly. I was afraid it might cost too much, but Missus Bradley just waved away my fears and bought it as well. The lid is decorated with porcupine quills and a tuft of moose hair. I think it quite grand. It is sitting here beside me now and I will tuck my journal away in it when I am done writing. The lovely smell of the sweet grass has filled up my entire bed nook.

But that wasn't the end of it. On the way home, as I had feared, Missus Bradley tired. I offered to run back and have the hotel send the pony trap for her, but she wasn't having any of that. She just sat down on a rock to rest and told me to sit beside her for a spell. I did and then she said to me, "Rosie, I just wanted you to know how pleased I am with your work. And so is Mister Bradley. You've been a great help ever since you arrived."

Then she added, her cheeks flaming bright red. "I think you may have suspected . . . We are going to have an addition to the family in November. Of course we will hire a nurse, but I know that you will be invaluable as well. Mary Margaret told me how good you were with the little ones at home."

And then she hugged me! I was that stunned. I could only stammer in reply and she must have thought me a right idiot.

Invaluable, she called me. Glowing, I am now. And I'm feeling all warm and happy inside to think that my big sister Mary Margaret spoke so highly of me. Still, she would have had to, wouldn't she? After all, wasn't it herself who persuaded Missus Bradley to take me on in the first place?

Tuesday, August 14th, 1866

Bossy Bessie and I are friends again. She came by for me this afternoon and asked me to go bathing with her. She started going on about Briney, and how she thought he was unsuitable as a friend, but before I could assure her that he was no friend of mine, she caught herself and changed the subject.

Now I am feeling guilty about being so quick to tell her that Briney wasn't a friend. I didn't actually say the words — she didn't give me time — but I *thought* them and I was going to. Briney has been so helpful, it seems ungrateful of me.

We had a grand time bathing and I even managed to swim a few strokes before sinking down and choking. I'll still not go out of my depth, though. It's reassuring to know I can put my feet down on the bottom whenever I want.

I suppose I should not be calling her "Bossy Bessie" anymore.

Wednesday, August 15th, 1866

The sunsets over the river are something wondrous. Missus Bradley and Bessie's mistress have become good friends as well and they spent the evening sketching the sun going down over the river. I thought Missus Bradley's sketch the finest; Bessie thought her Missus Forrester's far better. She would. I did not dare argue, however, as our friendship is still as fragile as a new shoot in the garden.

But Missus Forrester put far too much red in hers, she really did.

Wednesday, August 22nd, 1866

Mister Bradley and James have returned. We leave to go back to Ottawa tomorrow. I'm so sad! It's been grand here. Bessie and I have promised to see each other whenever we can. It will be nice to have a friend in Ottawa.

Friday, August 24th, 1866

I'm curled up in my berth on the steamer. No Missus Tubbs on this trip. In fact, I have my berth and the one next to it all to myself.

What a grand thing I have to write about tonight. I was in a state when we got near Québec City, knowing that I would be so close to my family again with no way to see them. I didn't say a word to Missus Bradley, of course, but she knew I was upset. She didn't seem too concerned about it, though, and I wondered at that. Lately she has been so kind.

When we arrived at the wharf I saw why. I had decided to stay below deck and not even look out, but Missus Bradley sent James down to ask me to come up. Of course I couldn't refuse, but it made me feel so bad that I was almost in tears. I found Missus Bradley at the rail and she was smiling.

"Look on shore, Rosie," she said to me. "Look who's waiting for you."

I looked, and there was my whole family! Mam and Da, Eileen, Bridget, Paddy, Mary Margaret and even Donny. I was that amazed I couldn't say a word. When the gangplank was let down I fairly flew into their arms. We all started talking at once, and Bridget was hanging onto my hand so tightly I thought it would be bruised. It wasn't until I had recovered my senses that I realized that Mam is expecting another babe too. At that, I felt a huge wave of guilt and worry sweep over me.

"Oh, Mam," I said. "How will you ever manage without me now?"

Then Eileen spoke up and said she would help Mam. I was about to retort that she wasn't more than a babe herself, but when I took a good look at her I suddenly saw that she's grown up in the months I've been away. She put her arm around Mam and I could see Mam lean into her the way she used to lean into me.

At first I felt nothing but relief, then the jealousy cut in. My stomach gave a sick kind of lurch. Was I so easily replaced? But Mam moved forward to give me a hug, and I saw the tears in her eyes, and I knew I wasn't. Then Paddy leaned over the edge of the dock so far that Mary Margaret had to pull him back, with a stern scolding, and we were all laughing again.

As we were going home, she took me aside. "Are you doing all right, Rosie?" she asked, and I was quick to answer that I was fine. Seeing her so happy, what else could I say?

I cannot begin to describe how I am feeling, everything is so mixed up between happy and sad, but it was grand to see them all.

Mister Bradley arranged it, can you believe that? He sent a note to Da telling him when we would be arriving at Québec City.

I think the Bradleys realized how devastated I was when we stopped on the way up. They might have felt sorry that they hadn't thought to let me off to see my family then, and wanted to make it up to me. In any case, it was nice of them to do that. Makes me think I am more appreciated now. More important.

Going back up the river, the steamer did take the canal past the rapids. I'm sure many of the passengers were pleased about that, but I wasn't.

Seeing my family was the best part of the trip

this time, but I don't know whether seeing them all again has made things easier or harder.

Monday, August 27th, 1866

We're back in Ottawa, and what a lovely surprise was waiting for Missus Bradley. Mister Bradley had arranged for her pianoforte to be shipped up from Québec and it was waiting for her when we arrived. Hardly enough room for it in the parlour, but she was so delighted, she didn't care. She sat down at it straightaway, took out her music, and began to play. She's been playing every moment she can ever since and this wee house is just filled with music. It's glorious, it is.

It will be grand for her now because she is beginning to show and soon will not be able to go out in society. It will give her something to do until the babe makes its appearance.

Tuesday, August 28th, 1866

Music is the only beautiful thing in this wretched house. It seemed so small and smelly after the hotel and fresh air of Cacouna and then, to make matters worse, we discovered that while we were away the drains got blocked and backed up. Cook was in a right state. We had to have men in to dig them up and clear them today. What a disgusting mess! It is horrible down in the cellar anyway. There's nothing but raised wooden slats for flooring and rats scurry around underneath them. I hear them squeaking and skritching around all the time and I will never go down there, but when the men dug up the drains the beasts just poured out all over the place.

Horrible horrible horrible!

At least I have this little room to myself. I have put my sweet grass box on a little table beside my bed. It is something pretty to look at, and the smell of the sweet grass is still strong. It helps.

Thursday, August 30th, 1866

Bessie made good her promise to come and see me and I'm almost wishing she hadn't. Didn't she just turn up her nose the moment I opened the door and greeted her. I was so happy to see her and, seeing as how Missus Bradley was napping and Cook was out shopping, I took her to the kitchen for a cup of tea. She looked around with her nose still up in the air and twitching as if something smelled bad (which, truth to tell, it does).

"Our house is much finer than this," she said.

Our house indeed! I was that riled I could have pushed her back out the door and shut it in her face. Nevertheless I buttoned my lip and served her the tea. She chattered on as if nothing was amiss and after a while I could not help but relent and chatter back.

Thanks be to all that's merciful she didn't come when the drains were being dug up.

Monday, September 3rd, 1866

Jean-Louis turned up this morning with a kitten for me! He said he had found it and thought I might like it. At least I think that's what he said. His English is still not too good.

A kitten! I've never had a cat before. Too many mouths in our house at home to feed as it was, so Mam discouraged any strays that came around. I was about to tell him there was no way I could take it, but he put it in my hands and the moment I felt the soft fluff of it I was lost. It doesn't weigh as much as a good pat of butter. All fur and big eyes it is. Grey and white, with a cunning wee pink nose. I stammered out a kind of thank you, but he was off again quick as a wink, and blushing bright scarlet. He must be the shyest boy I've ever seen.

But then I had to see if Missus Bradley would let me keep it. Cook was all for it. She said it would be good to have a cat around.

I gave it a saucer of milk and watched it lap it up, entranced with the sight of it. The tiny thing finished it all up — it must have been starving — then set in to cleaning itself. It cleaned its whiskers, one by one, then started in on every inch of its wee body. Cook and I couldn't help laughing at it, so seriously did it take itself.

Cook pointed out that it was a female and that would probably mean kittens next spring, but I didn't care. I'll find homes for them somehow.

When Missus Bradley came down for her tea, the little cat was curled up and purring so loudly I was certain she must have heard it from upstairs. I showed it to her and asked if I might keep it. I wanted to so much! I assured her that it would be very useful to have a cat around, as it might keep the rats down.

Missus Bradley just laughed and said I'd better keep it away from the rats. "The rats are twice as big as it is," she said. "They just might win that contest."

Still, she said the cat could stay.

I have named her Sophie.

Tuesday, September 4th, 1866

It might not be too long before Sophie is giving the rats a run for their money after all. She was drinking her milk in the kitchen this morning and nibbling at a piece of fish Cook had saved for her from yesterday's dinner, when in barged that idiot dog, Brutus. He saw Sophie and tried to put on the brakes, but just skidded clear across the room until his nose almost touched her. Did she run away? She did not. She fluffed her fur up to twice her size, arched her back, hissed at him and scratched his nose.

Brutus let out a yipe and ran out of the room. Didn't Cook and I laugh! Sophie just gave herself a shake and went back to eating her breakfast, as calm as could be.

Of course, the rats are probably much smarter than Brutus.

Tuesday, September 11th, 1866

Thank goodness the worst of the summer heat seems to be over now. Ottawa is much hotter than Québec. It's been hard on Missus Bradley, and I didn't like it either. The only one who doesn't seem bothered by it is Cook. Nothing seems to bother her, actually; she beams from morn to night. She does say she doesn't like the cold, though.

The air is much brisker these days, and some of the leaves are beginning to turn colour. I love this time of year. I'm just full of energy. Lucky that, because Missus Bradley has the house in a turmoil. Wants everything clean and tidy before the babe comes.

My kitten seems to think that the only place to sit is right on my journal where I cannot help but notice her. To make sure of it, she's batting my quill with her paw as I write. So far that has caused several blots on the page, so this will not be one of my neatest entries.

She is so funny I think I will finish this up and play with her.

Friday, September 14th, 1866

Work, work and more work. As if a newborn babe could take notice of how clean a house is.

Still, I suppose there will be a stream of visitors and well-wishers after the birth and Missus Bradley does not want to be shamed by a dirty house. It is a hard job to make this house clean, though. And the dog does not make it any easier. I have swept up bag after bag of dog hair and cleaned up after his muddy great paws more times than I care to count. Sophie is so much neater and tidier.

Brutus still gives her a wide berth. She takes full advantage of it and taunts him mercilessly. Last evening she even went so far as to sniff at his dinner dish. She wouldn't lower herself enough to eat out of it, of course — just teasing him, she was. The fool of a dog just stood there looking at her with the most worried expression I've ever seen on a dog's face. As soon as she sauntered off he was into the dish and slopping up the scraps as fast as he could. Sophie looked right disdainful. And so she should.

Monday, September 17th, 1866

I finally got up the nerve to ask Mister Bradley a question about this Confederation business. There is so much talk and buzz. I hear everyone going on about it when I'm out at the shops, and I get a bit more news when I read the papers before I tear them up at night, but truth be told, I really don't understand it. If it is the right thing for us, why are some people against it?

I waited until Mister Bradley was settled after

supper with his pipe and his newspaper and Missus Bradley had retired for the night. James had been dismissed for the evening, and Cook was off to visit her sister, so when I finished tidying up the kitchen I had a good opportunity to catch him alone without interruptions. I must admit I did not have the slightest idea of how to go about it, so I just plunged in and asked if he could answer a question for me.

Mister Bradley looked up at me and I could see he was surprised. I almost backed out then and scurried away, but I managed to meet his look.

"It's about this Confederation business," I managed to say. "I'm that confused about it all."

To my relief he didn't get annoyed, but said he would be happy to explain it to me. He even invited me to sit down to hear what he had to say.

I was so stunned I couldn't answer.

"Sit," he repeated. He sounded as if he were speaking to Brutus, and indeed the dog, who was lying quietly at his feet, looked up at him in puzzlement.

I sat.

Then he proceeded to give me a right good explanation. I still don't understand the whole of it, but perhaps if I write down what I can remember, it will help me fix it more clearly in my mind.

I knew that Mister John A. Macdonald, Mister George-Étienne Cartier and Mister D'Arcy McGee want to unite our Province of Canada with the Provinces of New Brunswick and Nova Scotia, but I had no idea as to how this was going to come about.

Mister Bradley told me that we have to have Great Britain's approval for this, as at the moment we are all British provinces. That is why Mister Macdonald and Mister Cartier are going to London in November to meet with the Queen to discuss the issue. They will be working on drafting an Act, called the British North America Act, which will create a brand new country of our own.

Mister Bradley thinks that in time Newfoundland and Prince Edward Island might join in the Confederation as well. He said that Mister McGee even sees the Colony of British Columbia joining some day, but that that's hardly likely because it's so far away.

I asked about Canada East, but he reassured me that there was little chance now that they wouldn't join in. That did make me feel better, but I still wish I could talk it out with Da. It's all a bit overwhelming.

Thursday, September 20th, 1866

My birthday today. I am fourteen years old. Not that anyone here knows it, nor am I about to tell them. My kitten is curled up on my bed with my old doll, Meggy. I'm remembering that Mam made that doll for me for my fourth birthday and I'm feeling right low and homesick. My first birthday away from home and everybody that I love.

But sure, what good is it to be sitting here feeling sorry for myself?

Friday, September 21st, 1866

Everyone knows about my birthday now! A great package arrived for me today by the post! Inside were notes from everyone in the family, even wee Paddy. And presents! Scones that Mam knows I love so well, a new pair of mittens for winter that she knitted for me, and a scarf that bears the scars of having been knitted by Eileen. Knitting is not her strong point, but I know how difficult it is for her and I shall cherish it all the more for the occasional holes and tangles in it. It will still be warm and cosy. Oat cakes from dear Bridget, who will be as good a cook as Mam some day. A round stone from Paddy, polished to a glow by the river. Just the sort of thing he loves and I'm sure is the pride of his collection. A new quill from Da, who knows how important this journal is to me, and a twist of lobelia seeds in a card from Mary Margaret. Lobelias are her favourite flowers and she writes in her note that these seeds are from her own garden. She likes to think that I will have them growing here to remind me of her. She drew a lovely scene of a garden just full of lobelias, and added a verse from an old Irish proverb that Grandmam used to quote:

May your troubles be less
And your blessings be more.
And nothing but happiness
Come through your door.

I will ask Missus Bradley for permission to plant the seeds next spring, right next to the front door. I will start them indoors after Christmas so they will be ready to go out in the garden after all danger of frost is over. They will make a grand showing there and I will think of Mary Margaret every time I look at them.

Then, after supper, Missus Bradley called me into the parlour and gave me a fine linen handkerchief with my initials worked into it. She must have embroidered it this very morning after the post came and she found out it was my birthday.

"And you shall have a day off all to yourself tomorrow," she said. "I sent a note round to Missus Forrester, and she's agreed to give Bessie the day off too, so the two of you can spend the day together."

Saturday, September 22nd, 1866

A grand day! The trees are in their glory across the river, all scarlet and gold shining against the blue of the sky. Bessie and I crossed over the bridge at the Chaudière Falls. We watched the rafts going down the slider for a while, then spent the rest of the day in the woods on the other side. Cook had packed up a lunch of bread and cheese, and we had all the fresh water we could drink from the springs flowing down from the hills. We picnicked at a spot high up where we could look back down at the river and the city beyond it. From there it looked so pretty, especially with the fine Parliament Buildings gleaming in the sun.

So I had a lovely birthday after all and I don't feel so sad. It's good to have a friend.

Monday, September 24th, 1866

My day of rest is just a memory. It's back to work, work and more work, although the house is gleaming already.

And wouldn't you know it, I spilled coffee this morning and some of it splashed onto James's shoes. It was only a small bit, but you would think I had soaked him from the knees down from the fuss he made.

"Useless girl," he snorted. It took every ounce of willpower not to snort right back at him. I am not used to being snorted at and I don't like it one bit.

Friday, September 28th, 1866

I can hardly bring myself to write this. Missus Bradley is ill. Terribly ill. And with the birth of the babe so near! The doctor has been round and we are all worried to death. He says she has an inflammation of the lungs. Living in this damp and smelly house, I am not surprised. Cook is making her broths and I am trying to get her to take a little, but her throat is sore and inflamed as well and she cannot get any nourishment down. Mister Bradley is beside himself. He has not gone to his office since she took ill.

Saturday, September 29th, 1866

Missus Bradley is no better. Briney asked how she was when he brought the water today. I wish I could have given him better news.

"Don't be despairing yet," he said, but I could tell it was just to keep my spirits up. Missus Bradley has always been good to him and he's as worried as the rest of us. More than once she has sent home leftovers with him, as she knows food is scarce in his house with so many mouths to feed there, not to mention that the Irish of Lower Town don't make much money.

Sunday, September 30th, 1866

I prayed as hard as I could at church today. Mister Bradley said that the minister at their church and the whole congregation prayed as well.

Monday, October 1st, 1866

The house is silent and grim. We tiptoe around, trying not to disturb Missus Bradley, and we talk in whispers, but I am feared that she is beyond hearing us. I have lived through much sickness with my sisters and brother — they have had their share of sore throats and inflammations, as have I, and we have all survived the mumps, thanks be to God, but I have never seen anyone this ill. The doctor is here every day, but nothing he does seems to help. Poor Missus Bradley is burning with fever. I will sit with her tonight, as Mister Bradley is so exhausted he cannot even think. The doctor has ordered him to bed but he will not leave her. He has had James move a couch into her room, and has given in to the point where he will lie down and sleep on it if I will sit by the bedside and keep watch. I am to rouse him immediately if there is any change.

I am so afraid.

Tuesday, October 2nd, 1866

Finally, I can write this with a joyous heart. The good Lord has seen fit to hear our prayers, and Missus Bradley will survive! I sat with her last night, despairing, as she tossed and turned and cried out all manner of nonsense. Then she fell into a deep sleep. I feared it was her last. I held her hand and stroked it, and then I realized that it was damp and not so hot as it had been. Sure enough, perspiration broke out on her forehead and she began to breathe more easily. I knew that meant the fever had broken. I roused Mister Bradley on the instant and we both sat with her until morning. I wiped her brow and kept applying cool cloths. This morning, for the first time since she fell ill, she opened her eyes and spoke to us.

I wept and so did Mister Bradley.

The doctor says she is out of danger now, but when I dared to ask about the babe she carries, he just shook his head.

"There's no way of knowing if the babe has been harmed by the fever or not," he said.

So we are not ready to celebrate yet. But, thanks be to God, Missus Bradley will live.

Wednesday, October 3rd, 1866

Missus Bradley has been able to swallow a few sips of Cook's broth. Cook is that pleased!

Thursday, October 4th, 1866

Missus Bradley is sitting up and eating bread and milk sops as well as broth. She is weak, of course, but her normal good spirits are returning to her.

Friday, October 5th, 1866

Mister Bradley insisted that I take myself out for a walk in the fresh air today. He said he didn't want me to fall ill as well.

"I don't know what we'd do without you, Rosie," he said.

It gave me a warm feeling around the heart to

know I am that appreciated here. I went out and had a grand walk, breathing in all the fresh, sun-filled air that I could, and brought back an armful of the glorious leaves. I put them in a jar and set it up on a dresser in Missus Bradley's room. She was so pleased with them.

It is good to see her healthy and smiling. We are none of us mentioning our fears for the babe, just taking as good care as we can of her. The doctor has given permission for her to sit out in the garden tomorrow if the weather stays fine.

Saturday, October 6th, 1866

Well, didn't Briney bring round a shepherd's pie today for Missus Bradley as a thank you for the left-overs. He said his mam made it, and she makes the best shepherd's pie in the world. Cook harrumphed at that, but the pie was grand. Missus Bradley ate a good, full meal for the first time since she took ill. She made certain not to offend Cook, though, by asking me to tell Cook that although it was good, it wasn't as good as hers. I did so, but made certain Briney was not around to hear me say it.

Now Cook is busy making a shepherd's pie of her own. She will not be outdone.

Monday, October, 8th, 1866

I made a wish on the new moon tonight. I wished that the words sent to me by Mary Margaret on my birthday would come true. A selfish wish, I know, but new moons are for wishing for yourself.

Wednesday, October 10ᵗʰ, 1866

Cook sent me out to Mister Buchanan's store on Sussex Street today. I love going to that store. It is so big! You must be able to buy anything in the world that you would want there. It's as grand as any grocery story in Québec City and as interesting as the store in Cacouna. I must admit, I did not hurry. It was a lovely day and it felt wonderful to be out in the sun. I had spent the morning stopping up cracks in the stove with wood ash and salt, wet with water, to keep it from smoking. Instead of praising me for making a good job of it, Cook just grumbled at the amount of salt I had used and sent me out for more. Perhaps sending me out on the errand was meant as a punishment, but if so, it was not. It was the brightest spot of my day.

Friday, October 12ᵗʰ, 1866

The talk is all of Mister Macdonald going to London, England, next month to see the Queen and decide our fate. Now that Mister Bradley has explained it to me, I understand more of what is going on.

❧

Sunday, October 14th, 1866

Missus Bradley is feeling well, but I think the babe will be coming within a month. I wonder how Mam is. Her babe is due not long after Missus Bradley's. I said a special prayer for her at Mass this morning and a prayer that Missus Bradley's babe will be hale and healthy.

Wednesday, October 17th, 1866

What a pickle!

That was a joke.

A man was driving a great cartload of pickles down Rideau Street today and one of the cart wheels hit a stump. Over went the cart and smash, smash, smash went all the pickles! All over the road.

Briney told me about it. We had a good laugh over it.

But in all truth, the state of the streets in this town is not amusing. They are a disgrace. And the sidewalks — when there are any — are worse. Cook and I were shopping at the market yesterday and she nearly took a terrible tumble. There's a place on Dalhousie Street where there's an open drain on one side and a great hole on the other. The sidewalk there is very narrow and because it had rained earlier on, it was that slippery! I had to hang onto her for dear life, although if she had lost her footing there was not much I could have done about it. She's a large woman, is Cook.

And don't talk to me about Sparks Street. With all the rain we had last week, there is mud up to the ankles and running water over the top and all around it. Cook and I saw a shop that has rigged up a canoe on the sidewalk in front of it with a great sign saying *Boats or Yachts for Hire.* Very funny.

But I was that muddy by the time I got home, I would have appreciated a boat.

Thursday, October 18th, 1866

A travelling menagerie is coming to town! The Hanlon Brothers' Circus.

Briney wants me to go with him to see it. I don't think I should spend the pennies that it would cost. I send almost all my wages home to Mam and Da every month, and a circus ticket seems like a terrible extravagance, but Briney is being very insistent. He is determined to go and to make me go with him. He even asked Missus Bradley on my part for the afternoon off on Saturday. That was a dreadful impudence, but Missus Bradley just laughed and said of course I must go.

Saturday October 20th, 1866

Oh, I am so glad that I went! Who could ever believe the things that I saw! I will sit here for a minute and breathe deeply, and then see if I can even begin to describe it.

To start off with, the Hanlon Brothers themselves

did the most amazing gymnastic feats. You wouldn't think people could contort themselves or leap around the way they did. What I liked best came next, though. A man named Professor W. Tanner, who had come all the way from England, had a troupe of the most adorable dogs and monkeys that did all kinds of tricks. I could have watched them all night. The program said that they had performed for Her Majesty Queen Victoria herself. Imagine that!

Then there was a beautiful lady who skated, dressed in a most dazzling costume, and another lady who did a kind of soldierly drill. And lots and lots of other acts. I came away with my head spinning and it has not stopped yet. Briney leaped around doing what he believed to be gymnastics, and made pretend sword thrusts, and even tried cartwheels in the mud all the way back to the house. I think people in the streets thought he had taken leave of his wits.

Cook gave us a glass of milk, but made him drink his outside because he was so muddy.

Wednesday, October 24th, 1866

My head was still in the clouds today, and didn't I go and scorch Missus Bradley's best collar when I was ironing it. I am totally humiliated. Sometimes I despair at how clumsy I am.

Thursday, October 25th, 1866

Missus Bradley found me weeping this morning and made me confess that I was upset about scorching her collar and afraid she would take the cost of it out of my wages.

She could not have been kinder and assured me that she had many more collars and she would be doing no such thing.

Now I feel even worse.

Wednesday, October 31st, 1866

The babe will be born this month. Missus Bradley is terribly uncomfortable. She spends most of her time in bed.

I wonder how Mam is doing? I'm sure Eileen is a great help, but oh how I wish I could be there. I'm sure she needs me, yet here I am so far away. I feel so useless!

Friday, November 2nd, 1866

Cook is making every kind of nourishing dish she can think of to tempt Missus Bradley's appetite. Missus Bradley can't seem to eat much, though.

How I wish I could send some of this wonderful food back to Mam!

Tuesday, November 6th, 1866

I don't know what is the matter with me. I cannot settle to anything, I am that worried about

Mam. I am missing her and Da and the little ones more than ever.

It is so cold today. The wind sneaks in through every crack in this drafty house. I am wrapped up in my quilt and I have Sophie on my lap. She's not really a kitten anymore, more like a young cat, and such a comfort to me. She, at least, is contented, and purring so loudly.

I wish I could show her to Bridget. She loves all animals and she would adore this kitten. I would have to keep her away from Paddy, though. He would probably chase her, just for the fun of it.

Monday, November 12th, 1866

Rained all day yesterday. The talk in the city is all about Mister Macdonald and his party going to London, and Mister Bradley is working long hours to help them prepare for it. No one else at our house cares a fig for that, though. The babe is surely due any day now and that is all we can think of.

Thursday, November 15th, 1866

More rain, although not so cold. When is that babe going to come? Missus Bradley keeps to her bed all the time now.

Friday, November 16th, 1866

The babe is here!!!! And a right lovely little boy he is. But my, what a time we all had! I don't have a moment to write more now, but I will tell all about it when things are back to normal.

Friday, November 23rd, 1866

I've just left Missus Bradley sipping a cup of warm milk and feeding baby Jonathan. He is such a darling — I'm smitten with him. But now to write down what happened.

Last Friday morning Mister Bradley had to go in to work because Mister Macdonald and the others were setting off for London. I knew he was uneasy about leaving Missus Bradley, but then, what can a man do to help with a birthing anyway?

It was a truly horrible day. No snow, but freezing rain and all sleety. Cook had gone to see her sister on Thursday and wasn't back yet, although she had only planned on going for the afternoon. She told us later that she had taken a tumble on the ice and fair knocked the senses out of herself, and her sister had insisted that she stay the night, she was that worried about her. So I was alone and just making a cup of tea for Missus Bradley when I heard her call out. I raced up the stairs and wasn't the babe coming!

"Fetch the doctor," she told me, but with Cook not being back yet, and James off with Mister Bradley, I couldn't leave her alone.

Just at that moment, I heard Briney's whistle outside. Truth, I was never so glad to see him in my life. I told him to run for the doctor and off he went. His da wasn't with him that day either, so he left the water cart and the horse tied to the fence.

I set a great pot of water on the stove to boil. That was what Missus O'Ryan did every time Mam had a babe, but truth to tell I wasn't too sure what it was for. Missus O'Ryan had always shooed me out of the house and told me to take care of the younger ones when we had a new one coming.

Then I went back up to sit with Missus Bradley

"Why have you not gone for the doctor, Rosie?" she asked me in a kind of gasp.

"Cook's not back yet," I told her. "I can't leave you alone. But Briney's gone," I added quickly when I saw her face fall. "He'll fetch him."

But didn't it take Briney nearly all morning to find him. It seems that Missus Bradley wasn't the only one giving birth to a babe on that day.

I sat with her and held her hand — it was all I could do — and kept the water on the boil. When Briney finally got back with the doctor, I was weak with relief.

"You're a good girl, Rosie," the doctor said to me. "You've done well. Now you can help me."

He sent me out of the room to heat quilts by the kitchen fire and keep the water boiling. Then there wasn't much I could do to help but just sit and wait. Briney finished delivering the water and then came back to wait with me.

At dinnertime Cook still hadn't arrived so I made soup out of all the boiling water. I didn't know what else to do with it.

At last I heard a squalling from upstairs and the doctor appeared.

"Tell Briney to go find Mister Bradley at the Parliament Buildings," he said. "He's got a fine boy and Missus Bradley is doing well. Bring those warm quilts up now, Rosie. And a bowl of that soup I can smell simmering on the stove for Missus Bradley, to help her recover her strength."

When Cook finally limped in, she was surprised to find it all over and done with. Mister Bradley is still beaming, he is so proud. That evening he called me up to Missus Bradley's room.

"Again, you were a great help," he said, and patted me on the shoulder.

I was looking over to where Missus Bradley lay cradling a bundle. She looked up at me and gave me a huge smile.

"Yes, thank you, Rosie," she said, and then she held the bundle out to me. "Would you like to hold the baby?" she asked.

Would I? Of course I would.

I remember holding Bridget and Paddy when they were newborn babes. I don't remember Eileen too well as I was not much more than a babe myself when she was born. But the others . . . Is there anything like holding a new wee babe in your arms and looking down into those wide, wondering eyes?

It's a miracle, it is.

God's own miracle.

Monday, November 26th, 1866

Missus Bradley is still in bed and I am helping out with baby Jonathan. Tonight he was fussing a bit and I was able to settle him. Missus Bradley says I have a way with babes. And well I should. I helped out often enough with Bridget and Paddy.

After the babe had finally fallen asleep, I was about to leave, but Missus Bradley bade me stay a while. Mister Bradley was working late and she did not want to be alone.

"Can you read, Rosie?" she asked me.

"I most certainly can," I replied, perhaps a little too indignantly. I was quick to catch myself and add in a more respectful tone of voice, "Yes, Missus, I can. I was considered a good reader at school."

She asked if I missed school. I was that surprised, for a moment I couldn't find words to answer her. Finally I mumbled, "Yes, Missus."

"I'm very tired tonight. Would you like to read to me?" she asked then.

I said I would and my heart lifted. I have not touched a book since I left school, and I miss it. She handed me a small volume. It was the poems of a person named Lord Tennyson.

"Read the one where I have the bookmark, then," she said. "'The Lady of Shalott'."

What can I say? I have never read words so beautiful in my life. Reading them was like water spilling from my mouth. When Missus Bradley saw how much I enjoyed it, she told me to take the book with me and read some more for myself. I could hardly believe it.

The Lady of Shalott is under a curse and must stay in one room, weaving, for all of her days. She is forbidden even to look out her window, but she has found a way to see what is going on in the world outside by looking at it in her mirror.

Here is some of what I read tonight. I think this is my favourite passage:

> *But in her web she still delights*
> *To weave the mirror's magic sights,*
> *For often thro' the silent nights*
> *A funeral, with plumes and lights*
> *And music, went to Camelot:*
> *Or when the moon was overhead*
> *Came two young lovers lately wed;*
> *"I am half-sick of shadows," said*
> *The Lady of Shalott.*

It is so sad. But somehow, I think I know exactly how she feels.

Tuesday, November 27th, 1866

They are hiring a nursemaid. It is to be expected, of course. Still, I have loved looking after wee Jonathan myself.

Friday, November 30th, 1866

The new nursemaid is here. Her name is Fanny and she is right bossy. She and Cook have already come to loggerheads. I have decided to keep out of her way as much as possible, but as I feared, I hardly see the babe at all. I am not needed nor wanted up in Missus Bradley's room now. I cannot help feeling a little hurt.

Sunday, December 2nd, 1866

Stir-up Sunday. Advent starts today. Cook is mixing up the Christmas pudding. It's made of beef suet, raisins, prunes and sugar. She packed it all in a pudding cloth, then dropped it in a pot of boiling water to cook. It will be served on Christmas Day after dinner, with a coating of brandy and a sprig of holly in the top. I've never seen this done before and am looking forward to a taste of it.

The altar at Mass this morning was draped all in purple. Father Guiliard preached that we should reflect on the First Coming of Christ at Christmas at this time of year, and look forward to His Second Coming.

I gave thanks for the blessing of this new babe, and added a special prayer for the safe arrival of my own mam's babe.

Thursday, December 6th, 1866

The first snow of the season! Not very much and it is gone already, but there will probably be more.

Saturday, December 8th, 1866

So much for snow. It rained all day today. The kitchen reeks of boiling nappies and they are strung all over to dry. As if the smell of the drains was not bad enough!

Wednesday, December 12th, 1866

Missus Bradley and baby Jonathan came downstairs today. James brought in armloads of wood and we built the fire up in the parlour until it was roaring. We settled the pair of them in a chair close to the hearth and I brought Missus Bradley a cup of warm, spiced milk.

It was good to see her downstairs, and her with such a good colour in her cheeks. The babe is thriving. He has a powerful pair of lungs on him, but of course I do not get to pick him up and settle him now. Fanny makes certain of that. She is a right pain, is our Mistress Fanny. I suppose I should not be saying that, but she is. Thinks she's the queen of the house. James is rather taken with her, but she cuts him dead. I am delighted to see that, but probably shouldn't be because it just makes him meaner than ever with me.

Thursday, December 13th, 1866

Still no more snow but it's freezing cold today. The house shudders in the wind and there is no keeping it warm. My little room is so cold that the water in my basin was frozen solid this morning.

Friday, December 14th, 1866

Missus Bradley is not receiving formally yet, of course, but Missus Forrester came by at teatime. She had been shopping, so she had Bessie with her to carry her bundles. After I served the tea, Bessie and I had a great time catching up on each other's news in the kitchen while our mistresses chatted in the parlour. James made certain to keep the fire up in there, and it was the only warm room in the house, with the exception of the kitchen — where the fires in the stove and the hearth are kept burning full blast — and Missus Bradley's bedroom. The rest of the house is unbearable.

Monday, December 17th, 1866

Cook is making the Christmas cakes. The smells of spices and good things baking have taken over from the drains and nappies. Halleluiah!

I am kept busy from morn to night. If I am not

running up and down stairs fetching clean nappies for the babe or warm milk for Missus Bradley, or building up the fire in her bedroom, I am recruited by Cook to stir and mix and watch the baking in the oven. Saints preserve me if I let anything burn, even if I am dashing madly about doing Mistress Fanny's bidding.

I was sent to Bates' grocery store this morning and I had a chance to look at the shop windows on Sparks Street. I do love them, especially at this time of the year. Mr. Bates has miniature steam engines in the window driving coffee and spice grinding machines. It is a wonder! And other windows are full of snowshoes and moccasins and all manner of winter wear. I had to buy tea for Cook too.

She loves her tea strong, does Cook. So strong you could trot a mouse across it, she says, although that is a vision I do not much appreciate. There are mice and rats enough in this house that it's all too likely to come to pass.

I think the most amazing thing of all, though, is the steam-driven rotary hairbrush in the window of Miles's Parliamentary Hairdressing Saloon. People were gawking in the window and talking about it. They say it will dry hair while the hair is being brushed.

I cannot imagine how it works, but it looks impressive. A bit dangerous, though.

Wednesday, December 19th, 1866

News from home! Mam has given birth to a wee boy. Timothy, his name will be. So now Paddy will be a big brother. He must be over the moon with pride.

I sent back a blanket that I quilted for the new babe, but oh how I wish I could deliver it and wrap it around baby Timmy myself. Still, I must content myself that all went well and Mam and babe are safe and healthy.

Fanny had an afternoon off today and I actually got to hold baby Jonathan again. He has grown marvellously. I fancied he gave me a smile. I know it was just gas, but in my heart I felt it was a smile and I smiled right back at him.

Friday, December 21st, 1866

Mister and Missus Forrester are invited to share Christmas dinner and they will bring Bessie with them to help out. It will be a grand affair. Cook has me running back and forth to the market every day, sometimes twice a day, and the kitchen is in a state. Food is boiling, stewing, simmering, being chopped, being mixed — everything all at once. The smells are glorious. I should feel right tired with it all, but I don't. It's exciting, that's what it is, and I love being a part of it.

Sunday, December 23rd, 1866

Church was lovely today, decorated with boughs of pine and holly, and the smell of incense filling every nook and cranny. I love going to Mass, and most especially at Christmas time.

Monday, December 24th, 1866

To our surprise, Jean-Louis turned up this morning with a basket of dried cranberries. Jean-Louis is still shy, but a sweet boy. He is learning a few more words of English and at the same time I am learning a few more words of French, so we are beginning to be able to talk to each other.

Cook was pleased and showed me how to make cranberry sauce after we soaked the cranberries in water all morning.

Here is the recipe:

> 1 teacup of water, 3 teacups full
> of cranberries, and a whole scandalous
> cup and a half of sugar.

We mixed them all up, put them on the stove, and boiled them very gently until the cranberries popped open.

Cranberries are very sour and that is why they take so much sugar, but I was aghast. Mam would never use that great an amount.

All is in readiness for dinner tomorrow. Here is our menu:

A boned turkey with a boned chicken
inside it
Cranberry sauce
Smashed turnips (I could do without
that!)
Roast potatoes

I could write a whole journal describing how Cook boned the turkey (with my help, I must add), and how all the remaining spaces inside the birds were filled with stuffing. It will be a masterpiece.

For dessert there will be cake, the Christmas pudding that Cook made on Stir-up Sunday, and sweets.

And elderberry wine! Not that I will get to taste that, I'm sure.

Sad it is, though, that although it has been right cold there is no snow to speak of. Instead of a white winter wonderland, we have slippery, frozen mud to make our way through for the Christmas Eve services.

No time to write more. I will describe it all after Christmas Day when I get the time.

Thursday, December 27th, 1866

Finally! Snow! And a fair amount of it. Mister Bradley was off to work this morning, but I'm sure he must have had a hard time of it, trudging through the drifts. The rest of us are tucked into the house, trying to stuff up cracks and keep the drafts out, and keeping the kitchen and the parlour fires burning.

Jean-Louis turned up with firewood this morning, bless him. He had the horse pulling the sleigh for the first time this year. James had gone off with Mister Bradley, so Jean-Louis carried several loads of wood right into the house for us. Cook was so grateful she gave him a package of leftover turkey to take home to his family. By the look on his face I knew that it was much appreciated. I fear his Christmas was not as sumptuous as ours.

Then Briney turned up with the water and that was welcome too, as most of the water we had on hand was frozen. He had the barrels covered in blankets. Cook also gave him a package of turkey, and I am sure he was just as grateful.

It is fearful cold in my room and I am bundled up in my quilt. Sophie is on my lap, purring, and we are both warming each other. My fingers are half frozen, but I must write all about our festivities.

On Christmas Day, Cook and I had everything ready when Mister and Missus Forrester arrived after church. While they were shown into the dining room, Bessie came into the kitchen and we set to work.

James served at the table, Fanny kept the babe quiet upstairs. The meal was grand. A feast it was. The pudding was just as delicious as I had hoped, and I got a generous piece of it.

When all was done they moved into the parlour where we had a roaring fire burning. James served them the elderberry wine in there. Cook finally sat down to rest — her ankle that she turned last month was bothering her — and allowed herself a glass of the elderberry wine as well. Bessie and I did the washing up. A fair job that was, but we were so happy to have the time together that we didn't mind one bit. When we finished, Cook gave us each a cup of eggnog. That was delicious. I savoured every sip, and it made me quite dizzy.

All went well, although we did nearly have one crisis. James had brushed Brutus till his fur shone for the occasion and Missus Bradley had tied a red bow to his collar. He behaved very well for once and was lying quietly at the dining room door when Sophie decided that she should make an appearance too. She walked into the room, tail waving, and passed right by Brutus's nose, fully aware that she was taunting him. He rose to the challenge and scrambled to his feet, fur bristling. Thanks be, at a sharp word from Mister Bradley, he settled back down, although he was scowling as only a dog can scowl, and I rushed to pick Sophie up and shut her back up in my room, but it could have been a disaster.

I wonder how Mam and Da and the little ones celebrated Christmas. I have not been able to stop thinking about them. Our Christmasses were never so grand as this one, but oh, how we enjoyed them. We would go to Mass on Christmas Eve and then come home to a cup of hot cider. No turkey for us, but Da would usually manage to buy us a good chicken and no one can roast chicken as well as Mam. I miss them all so much!

Monday, December 31st, 1866

The last day of the year. What will 1867 bring? I wish I could believe that it would bring a chance for me to visit home, but that is not likely.

Tuesday, January 1st, 1867

Yet another scouring out of the house to greet the New Year spick and span.

Thursday, January 3rd, 1867

What the New Year has brought me is a horrible cold. I am so miserable I can do nothing, not even write in this journal.

Thursday, January 17th, 1867

A full fortnight I've been ill and confined to my bed. Today I was able to get up for a bit, but I'm so weak I have to sit down every minute or so. I have not ever been so ill, not even when I had mumps. Cook was so good to me, although I thought her remedies would be the end of me. The cold went into my chest and I coughed so much I thought I was turning inside out. She made mustard plasters and kept them on my chest, and right nasty things they are. Cloth bags filled with a paste made of mustard and heated up as hot as I could stand it and then some. Near burned my skin off, they did, and I near died with the smell and the heat of them, but I guess they did the trick, as I did get better.

Monday, January 21ˢᵗ, 1867

This New Year is becoming worse and worse. No sooner had I recovered from my illness than I came down with a toothache. Missus Bradley took me to the dentist and he pulled the tooth. I will not even try to describe the pain of that. He gave me brandy to ease the pain, but all that did was make me sick. I was abed again for a day recovering. Back to work today, but still feeling weak and wobbly and my mouth hurts so that I cannot eat.

It is snowing again and I am feeling so miserable I wish I could just curl up in my bed, draw the quilt over my head, and do nothing but cuddle Sophie and Meggy until spring. What a dream that would be!

Wednesday, January 23ʳᵈ, 1867

This evening Mister Bradley brought home news from London. The British North America Act is coming along and no one is opposing it, so it does seem as if everything will work out, but there was also unsettling news. Mister Macdonald was seriously burned in his hotel room when a candle set fire to a chair he was asleep in. He is said to be attending the sessions of the conference nonetheless, but in great pain.

Monday, January 28th, 1867

I was well enough to go to Mass yesterday. It snowed again on Saturday, so the walking was difficult, but I was so sick of being in the house I was determined to go and I'm glad I did. Today is sunny and bright. The city looks almost pretty with all the mud covered in a layer of white and the snow sparkling in the sunlight.

I am feeling much better. It was Bessie's free day and she came by. She has great plans to go skating on the river now that it has frozen. I do not have skates, though, so don't fancy I will be able to do that.

Tuesday, January 29th, 1867

It looks like I'm going skating after all! Missus Bradley heard me telling Bessie I didn't have skates here with me, and didn't she offer to lend me hers. Said she wouldn't be using them this winter. She thought they might fit and they do. Almost. They are a little big, but I have wadded some cotton up in the toes and that helps. We're making plans to go on Saturday next, as it's a free day for both Bessie and me. I'm so excited, I can barely wait. Bessie says she is a good skater. I am not, but I did skate a bit in Québec City, so I can at least stand up and not fall about too much.

Wednesday, January 30th, 1867

Briney is coming too. He's going to borrow his big brother's skates.

Saturday, February 2nd, 1867

Well, we went skating, and what a tale I have to tell now.

Just as we were getting ready to go, Jean-Louis turned up. Briney had invited him to come along with us, so we were a merry foursome that set off. It snowed this morning, but not much, and by the time we left it had stopped and the sun came out. It was not even too cold.

We went down to the river behind the Parliament Buildings and put on our skates there, leaving our boots hidden behind some rocks. I was doubtful about doing this, as I dearly needed those boots and could not afford to replace them if they were stolen, but Briney assured me that he did this all the time.

"There are probably boots hidden all over the place around here, if you wanted to search them out," he said.

We had a fine time, although those two foolish

boys were right idiots. We were skating along quite happily and enjoying the sun and the breeze out on the river, and I had only fallen twice, when Briney found a stick and began batting a rock around. Well, of course there was nothing for it but Jean-Louis had to find a stick and start battling Briney for possession of the rock. That was the end of our quiet, peaceful skate. The two of them wouldn't let up their foolish game. They tried to encourage Bessie and me to find sticks and take part in it, but we were having none of it. We skated on, but the boys got more and more excited and carried away.

Suddenly, Bessie and I realized that they were skating perilously close to the middle of the river. We could see a patch of open water right close to them, where the current was the strongest. We yelled at them, but they were making so much noise they couldn't hear us. I started to skate out to them, to warn them, but Bessie held me back. We shouted some more and finally they heard us.

"Water!" I screamed and pointed. "Open water!"

At that they looked up and realized where they were and the danger they were in. Didn't they just race back then, but even so they never let up batting at the rock all the way.

"The pair of you will be the death of me!" I fair screamed at them when they at last reached safety. "Are you both daft?"

Oh, I was that riled!

They had the grace to look shamed, but that only lasted a moment or two and then they were back at it again. Nonetheless, we had a grand day and the boots were still there when we returned.

We all walked back to Mister and Missus Bradleys' house and Cook made us hot cider to warm us up.

Wednesday, February 6th, 1867

Terrible news today. Mister Bradley read out from the newspaper that a lady from town disappeared during a skating party last evening and is feared drowned. It seems that her party skated far down the river and it began to get dark before they could get back. Somehow or other this poor woman got separated from the rest of them. Her friends searched and searched for her as long as they could, and searchers went out again as soon as it was daybreak, but they could find no trace of her. It's said that she must have fallen through and the current carried her body under the ice.

I shudder when I think how close those foolish boys came to the same fate.

Monday, February 11th, 1867

Dull, clammy weather.

Wednesday, February 13th, 1867

Not so cold today. Still, spring seems so far away.

Monday, February 18th, 1867

What a horrible month February is! The wind is enough to drive a body mad.

Wednesday, February 20th, 1867

I am that discouraged I can barely bring myself to write in this journal. If the sun does not shine soon I think I will break down in tears.

Monday, February 25th, 1867

Fanny is off home to visit her sister and I am nursemaid again. I had baby Jonathan to myself and I made the most of it. I love nuzzling my face into his neck and just breathing in the smell of him. There is nothing like the smell of a clean and freshly washed babe.

Of course there is nothing like the smell of a babe who has soiled himself either, but I suppose we have to take the bad with the good.

In any case, for two days I have revelled in caring for him. Missus Bradley says I am a wonderful nursemaid. And why wouldn't I be? I had enough practice with the little ones at home when they were new born. But caring for Jonathan makes me think about baby Timothy. He will grow up without me ever knowing him!

Now I've made myself homesick again. Will I ever get over missing home and my family? I'm so far away from them, and all their life is going on without me. I suppose I'm missing them even more because it was little Paddy's birthday today and I was not there to make him his favourite treat, apple hedgehog, made out of dried apples and sugar boiled up together. After it cooled, I used to stick almond slivers all over it to look like the quills of a hedgehog, and then decorate it with gobs of whipped cream. Oh, how he loved it.

I expect all the family was there to help him celebrate. Probably even Mary Margaret, there with the rest of them, while because of her I am so far away and so alone. It is still hard, sometimes, not to be resentful.

Thursday, February 28th, 1867

The last day of February, the Lord be praised. If this had been a year when there was an extra day in this wretched month, I could not have borne it.

I am so sad and lonely. I cannot think of anything but home. This morning I was so preoccupied that I dropped a whole bowl of porridge at breakfast time. Clumsy again. Cook scolded me, as well she might, and I just dissolved into a flood of tears. I cannot believe that I will ever be happy again. Foolish thoughts, I know, but I cannot help myself.

Cook has an earache, which doesn't improve

her temper. She is walking around with an onion poultice in the ear. I hope it helps.

Monday, March 4th, 1867

We had a dreadful accident today. Much worse than dropping a bowl of porridge. And this time I came out of it a hero rather than a ninny. I'm still not quite certain how.

I was throwing out the slops after breakfast when I smelled smoke. I looked around and sure enough, smoke was coming out of the cowshed. At that moment Daisy began to low and I could hear her thrashing around. I ran over to the shed and threw open the door, only to be greeted with a wall of smoke that blasted me in my face. Daisy was distraught.

I dashed in to try and lead her out, but I didn't have a rope with me and that foolish beast was having none of it. I think she'd got it in her head that I was the cause of it all. She backed away from me as far as she could and thrashed her head from side to side. I could not get a grip on her.

At that very moment I saw flames licking at the back wall. You would have thought that would send the cow out the front, but not a bit of it. It just increased her frenzy. Finally, in desperation, I grabbed onto her ear with one hand and threw my other arm around her neck. I pulled as hard as I could, but she still wouldn't do my bidding. Then I remembered something I had heard about leading horses from a flaming barn — their eyes should be covered. I whisked off my shawl and bound it over her eyes, then resumed my pulling. At last she gave in and let me drag her out, quite literally by the ear.

By the time I got her out, James had noticed the smoke and was there with a bucket of water, and Cook not far behind carrying another. They ran back for more and were so enthusiastic in putting out the blaze that they did not quite wait for the cow and me to emerge completely. We both got a soaking. Not too bad for Daisy, but I did not appreciate it.

Be that as it may, did Mister and Missus Bradley not come down into the kitchen and praise me as a hero?

Much better than being scolded as a dolt who spills porridge.

Mind you, once the whole affair was over and the fire had been safely put out, Cook could not help laughing at me for dragging the beast out by the ear.

Wednesday, March 6ᵗʰ, 1867

Today is Ash Wednesday, the beginning of Lent. What should I give up for Lent this year? Truth be told, I do not have that much that I can spare anything. And I have been that sad lately, I do not wish to make my lot any harder than it is.

That is not a very Christian way of thinking, though. Surely there is something.

Later

I will give up tea. Tea is very comforting to me and I will miss it.

Sunday, March 10th, 1867

First Sunday in Lent. Our priest spoke about sacrifices for Lent and how much greater was the sacrifice of our Lord in giving us His Son to save us from our sins. It made me think my small sacrifice of tea is not so great after all.

Still, I will miss it.

Wednesday, March 13th, 1867

Briney says the sap is beginning to run. He and his younger brother Kevin are going to tap some trees and make maple syrup. He will take me out to see and taste it on my next free day.

Mister Bradley continues to give us news as to how negotiations are progressing in London for the passing of the British North America Act that will give us our constitution. It has passed the House of Lords and on March 8 passed the House of Commons.

The most surprising news, though, is that Mister Macdonald has been wed in London! The lady who is now his wife is Agnes Bernard, the sister of Mister Macdonald's private secretary. Everyone in Ottawa is agog over the news and waiting to see what she is like when Mister Macdonald brings her back here.

Friday, March 15*th*, 1867

We are going to Briney's sugar bush Saturday next.

Friday, March 22*nd*, 1867

Didn't Jean-Louis turn up with a whole barrel of maple sap today! Cook is going to boil some up and show me how to make maple-sugar pie.

Saturday, March 23*rd*, 1867

Briney came by this morning to take me out to the sugar bush he and his brother have tapped. He was furious when he saw the barrel of sap beside our kitchen door that Jean-Louis had brought. I do believe that fool of a boy was jealous.

In any case, I placated him somewhat by going with him for the day and we had a grand time. I had never seen trees tapped before, although I love the syrup that the sap makes when it's boiled up.

Kevin had already boiled up some sap in the lean-to they had out there when we arrived and we had a great time pouring the hot syrup into the snow to make maple taffy.

Wednesday, March 27th, 1867

Cook and I made maple-sugar pies today. Here is the recipe for one pie, but thanks to Jean-Louis we had such an abundance of sap that we made several.

First we boiled a great quantity of sap down until it went past the syrup stage to make maple sugar. Then Cook made enough pastry for several pies. I was in charge of rolling it out and spreading it in the pie tins. Then we made the filling:

> 1 cup and a quarter cup more
> of maple sugar
> A scant cup of freshly churned cream
> 2 eggs, well beaten
> 1 generous pat of butter
> Cook all the ingredients together
> until they get nice and thick.
> Cool them, then pour them into
> pastry-lined pie tins and bake.

My job was to beat the eggs.

We made pies for the household, then one for Jean-Louis as a thank you for the sap, and one for Briney so that he would not feel left out. They were the most delicious things I have ever tasted.

I'm right glad I did not give up maple syrup for Lent.

✤

Friday, March 29th, 1867

You will never imagine what that cow did today.

The barrel of maple sap was on the back kitchen stoop. We kept it covered, but somehow or other, the lid fell off. Didn't Daisy get out of her stall, discover it and drink a great quantity of it!

The first we knew of it was later this afternoon when we heard a bellowing and lowing as if the cow were in distress, as she most certainly was. The sap had caused her stomach to distend hugely and she was in great pain. Mister Bradley called immediately for the veterinarian, but it was at least two hours more before he was able to come.

"We must pierce her stomach to let the gas out," he said. I could not believe it, but watched in horror as he pulled out a sharp dagger and thrust it through a thick piece of wood until only about four inches of the blade protruded. They tethered Daisy securely and Mister Bradley and James held her head while the veterinarian made ready to stab her.

I couldn't watch, but I couldn't not watch.

The veterinarian drew back his arm and stabbed at poor Daisy's swollen side with all his might. The piece of wood stopped the blade from going in too far, and Daisy's distended stomach deflated with a great *whoosh* and a horrible smell. I thought she would be in agony, but quite the opposite. Didn't she just give a huge sigh of relief and immediately stop her bellowing.

When James shut her up in the shed (now repaired from the fire) for the night, she seemed completely back to normal, although she is not being allowed anything to eat for a day or two.

Through it all Sophie sat on the back stoop and watched with interest and not a little disdain for the stupidity of cows. Brutus was nowhere to be seen. I think he was in hiding, perhaps fearing he was next for the treatment.

Tuesday, April 2nd, 1867

When Mister O'Grady came by with the water barrels this morning Briney was not with him. Kevin was helping his da instead. When I asked him where Briney was he told me that their older brother, Thomas, who works at the mill, had had a terrible accident. He broke his leg very badly when a timber fell on him. He will be laid up for some time, so Briney has gone to work in his stead. They cannot take the chance that he will lose his position.

I'm so worried about the foolish boy. The mill is a dangerous place. Mister O'Grady is worried too, I can tell, but he didn't say anything. I know the family needs the income from that job. There is another younger brother and two little girls in the family as well, so money is scarce, even though the two older girls work. Kevin is only twelve, but I expect he has left school so as to help out.

Wednesday, April 3rd, 1867

I'm worried about Briney.

Thursday, April 4th, 1867

I'm so troubled about Briney I cannot think of anything else. Mister O'Grady is not due to come by with the water until next week, though, so I expect I won't hear anything until then.

Saturday, April 6th, 1867

What a relief! Didn't Briney come by this evening to let me know how things stand. He came straight from the mill and I have never seen him so dirty or so tired. He started apologizing for his appearance and was carrying on about it until I hushed him and told him to pay it no mind and to let me know how he was handling the work at the mill and how his brother was doing.

First of all, I think he actually enjoys the work at the mill, the foolish boy. He sounded very proud of himself and the more he told me about it and the more worried I became about it, the prouder he got. Why are boys so daft?

Unfortunately, Thomas is not doing well. His leg is not healing and the doctor who came to set it was not very encouraging about it. Briney says the leg is broken in two places and the doctor is afraid Thomas will never walk properly again.

If Thomas cannot walk, he surely cannot work.

I wonder what will happen? The family desperately needs his wages.

Wednesday, April 10*th*, 1867

The ice is off the river now and spring does seem to be coming. It has been such a long, hard winter.

No more news from Briney. I'm so anxious about him.

News today from London, though. On the 29th of March (the very day Daisy had to be stuck with a knife to relieve her bloating) Queen Victoria gave our bill her royal assent. Mister Bradley is elated.

"We are well on our way to being our own country!" he said tonight.

Saturday, April 13*th*, 1867

Thanks be, Briney came around again today. He had the afternoon off and was going fishing and asked if I might go with him. Missus Bradley gave me leave for a couple of hours and off we went.

I would have enjoyed the outing if Briney had not been so worried about Thomas. His leg is still not mending well. At least Briney caught a great many fish, and that made him happy. He said his mam would be glad of them to help out with their meals. I think they cannot afford meat or fish from the market too often.

I even caught some fish! Briney showed me

how to hold the rod and set the hook when I saw a fish take it. I would not put the worm on, though. I caught several perch and Briney said they were right good eating. I wouldn't take them off the hook either, so Briney had to do that. I did not like them thrashing around and they were far too slimy and slithery to hold.

We caught several buckets full of fish, including sunfish and rock bass as well as the perch. We saw a huge muskie swim by, but it ignored us regally.

When we were done I offered to help carry the buckets home with Briney. At first he refused — I think he was embarrassed to have me see his home — but the buckets really were too cumbersome for him to manage by himself, so in the end he gave in.

His house is little more than a shack down by the river in Lower Town. The street is really just a path, even muddier than ours. When we came up to the door, Briney's two little sisters came running out. They are sweet girls and put me much in mind of Bridget. They were shy with me at first, but soon became easy and by the time I left they were hanging onto my skirts.

Briney's mam is lovely. She was so pleased with the fish. In spite of my protests, she wrapped up several of the perch for me to take back to the Bradleys.

"There's plenty for all," she said, "and it's a right feed we'll have tonight."

She insisted, too, on giving me a slice of bread

and butter — to keep my strength up in the cool of the evening. She offered me tea, as well, but I explained I had given it up for Lent. When I left she gave me a great hug and it was all I could do not to burst into tears, it made me miss my own mam so.

Briney was right about Thomas, though. He was lying on a pallet by the kitchen fire and he does not seem well at all. He just lies with his face to the wall and will not talk. Briney says Thomas is desperate about the fact that he may not be able to work again.

Cook was pleased about the perch. She rolled them in flour and fried them up in butter and we had a glorious feed too.

Sunday, April 14th, 1867

Palm Sunday today. I said a special prayer for Thomas.

Wednesday, April 17th, 1867

I have had the most exciting news! Missus Bradley called me in to the parlour this morning and asked me if I would like to visit my family in Québec City! It seems Mister and Missus Forrester are travelling to the city after Easter, as Missus Forrester has a sister there and she wishes to visit her. They are taking Bessie and offered to take me as well. I will be away for two weeks and will have to make up for it with fewer days off when I get back, but it will be worth it.

I am beside myself with joy.

Thursday, April 18th, 1867

Maundy Thursday today. The end of Lent. I can drink tea again but, truth be told, I am so excited about going home that I can't even think about that.

Friday, April 19th, 1867

Good Friday. It was hard for me to keep a solemn face today at Mass. It would not have done for me to be smiling on such a sad day, but it was all I could do to keep the happiness covered up inside me.

I'm going home!

Saturday, April 20th, 1867

Briney came by late this evening. He came straight from his work at the sawmill and I was shocked at his appearance. He has become so thin! I was glad to see him, though, and told him my good news.

He said he would miss me. At that, didn't I get right shy. I wanted to say I would miss him too, but the words wouldn't come out. We spoke a bit longer, then he said he had to be getting off home. Things were a little strange between us. Not like they usually are. He seems older somehow.

I will miss him, but I am so excited about the trip I cannot really think of anything else.

Sunday, April 21st, 1867

Easter Sunday. At last I can let my excitement out. I must admit that the joy for the glorious Resurrection of our Saviour is much mixed with my own private delight. I surely hope that is not a sin. I will ask the priest at my next confession.

Next week! We leave next week on the train to Québec City!

Tuesday, April 23rd, 1867

We leave today. I have my bundle packed and ready. I did not sleep a wink last night.

Friday, April 26th, 1867

I am sitting curled up in my old corner of the children's room. Bridget is snuffling and snoring softly on her pallet, as she always did. Paddy is fast asleep and Eileen is snuggled up close beside me. I cannot begin to describe how warm and happy I feel. I cannot write much now, but I will set down a few words about the trip here.

Bessie and I sat together on the train and had a grand visit. That girl is never at a loss for words. She talked the whole way, except when we were sleeping. Even then she talked in her sleep a bit. Missus Forrester is a lovely lady. Cook had given me some bread and cheese, but Missus Forrester had a big hamper with all manner of delicious provisions. She shared it liberally with Bessie and me before she and Mister Forrester transferred to the sleeping car on the train from Montreal to Pointe Levi. I am still a little shy in Mister Forrester's presence, but he buried himself behind a newspaper for most of the time when we were travelling together.

My opinion of travelling on the rail cars has not changed. I opened the window to catch a breeze and promptly got a cinder in my eye. I did not need Missus Forrester's admonition to shut it very quickly.

How very noisy, dirty and uncomfortable it is to travel by train.

But never mind. It does get you where you want to go. And here, back at home, is most definitely where I wanted to go.

When the ferry docked in Québec City, there was my whole family waiting for me. I began to weep, and wept all the way home.

Enough for now. I am going to curl up close to Eileen and just delight in the dear, familiar smell of her and of home.

I will continue tomorrow.

Sunday, May 5th, 1867

I cannot believe I have not written a word in this journal in the whole two weeks that I have been home. And now it's time to leave! Where has the time gone?

In living and delighting to be back with my family, that is where. Again, I am tucked up in my bed, as I was in my last entry, but how different I'm feeling now. Sad, that's what I am, that this visit is over. Still, I can't be too sad, for it has been lovely. I will have the memories warm in my mind for months to come.

First of all, baby Timothy. What a delight! He is round and fat and full of giggles and chortles. I have not been able to get enough of him. And Mam looks well and hearty. She has recovered from the birth, which she said was easy, although I have a hard time believing that. Birthing is never easy, it seems to me.

And more good news — Mary Margaret is expecting a babe of her own now. She and Donny have been over to visit as much as they could and it is so good to be a little sister again instead of always trying to be old and competent. Indeed, I have been petted and made much of, to such an extent that I fear I am spoiled.

Finally, I was able to have a good talk with Da about Confederation, and I was not surprised to hear that he is all for it. A country must go forward, he said, and we can only do that if we unite. When I asked him if he was worried about Canada East not joining in, he told me not to fret about that. He said some people were against it, but most, English and French, felt as he did. He even thought that being together within a larger independent country might bring the two peoples closer together.

But it's back on the train tomorrow. Mister and Missus Forrester will be by to pick me up. I have asked Mam and Da not to go to the ferry. I want to say goodbye here at home.

The strangest thing has happened, though. I could not have loved being back at home more, but it's different, and I have had a hard time puzzling it out. Da seems older, quieter. Eileen has become so grown up and responsible, Mam depends on her now so much. Bridget isn't the baby she was when I left. She was fair bubbling over with stories about school and the best friend she has made there. Although she hugged me as tightly as ever, I could tell that she didn't really need me as much as she used to. Mary Margaret is wed and will have her own family now. Even wee Paddy, after the first rush of welcoming me home, was off with his friends and little it was that I saw of him from then on.

For a little while, in spite of the spoiling, I felt left out — as if I weren't really part of the family any more. But of course I am, and just as well-loved as ever. But things have changed. They've all moved on without me just fine.

That's as it should be, I know. At least, that's what I tell myself.

Wednesday, May 8th, 1867

Back in Ottawa. The smell of the sawmills hit me as soon as I stepped off the train. It is raining, muddier than ever, and the drains are blocked up again.

It's very late. I have not the heart to write more.

Thursday, May 9th, 1867

The Bradleys are very pleased. The cornerstone of their new church was laid today. It is to be called St. Alban's.

Sure enough, Sophie has had kittens. Now I must find homes for them when they are old enough. Bessie has asked permission from Missus Forrester and will take one, Cook says her sister will take two. To my surprise, Jean-Louis has said that he will take one. His mam has always had a cat and hers just died. He said it would be a great comfort to her. I am sure I will find homes for the rest as well. They are so wee and cunning, and Sophie is being a good mother to them. I could sit and watch them for hours, but of course Cook will have none of that.

Friday, May 10th, 1867

There has been a sawdust explosion and fire in the mill where Briney is working! Two men have been injured.

No news of Briney. I am beset with worry!

Saturday, May 11th, 1867

Still no news of Briney. The two men who were injured have died.

Sunday, May 12th, 1867

Briney is all right!

I can breathe properly again. I was in such a state that I was totally useless helping Cook prepare dinner after Mass today. I kept dropping things and forgetting things. Finally Cook got so annoyed with me that she asked Missus Bradley if I could be let off to go and find out about Briney.

Needless to say I was out of the house like a shot and ran the whole way to Briney's. To my relief, it was Briney himself who answered my knock at the door. I am still embarrassed to say that I threw my arms around him in a great hug. He didn't seem to mind, and hugged me back.

I am distressed, though, because he is going back to work there tomorrow. He says that with Thomas still abed, the family needs the wages. He said that Thomas is not healing well and will probably never be able to work in the mill again, and he is planning on staying there permanently.

I was horrified, but he said he felt it was his duty. I argued that his father needed him to help deliver the water, but he told me that Kevin has left school and will take his place there.

Nothing I could say would change his mind and

I'm sorry to say that we had a fair set-to and parted very coolly after the argument.

Thomas was lying on his cot in the corner of the kitchen by the hearth during all this, but he kept his face to the wall and didn't say a word. It's only now that I think of it that I realize that of course he heard every word, and how terribly embarrassing it must have been for him.

I wish I could take back some of the things I said, but of course I can't.

Monday, May 13*th*, 1867

Mister Macdonald and Mister Cartier and the others who went with them are back from London. The town is all agog with excitement over Mister Macdonald's new wife. Mister Bradley saw her and says she is a pleasant-enough looking woman. He added that he hoped she knew what she was in for. I have heard that Mister Macdonald can be a difficult man at times — I suppose that is what Mister Bradley meant, although he didn't realize I was listening — and he added that Mister Macdonald sometimes has a problem with drink.

Tuesday, May 14*th*, 1867

I am worried about Briney, but can do nothing about it.

Friday, May 17th, 1867

Still no news from Briney. I wonder how he is doing.

Monday, May 20th, 1867

Mister O'Grady and Kevin came by to deliver the water today. I rushed out to pepper them with questions about Briney, but Mister O'Grady stopped me in mid-rush.

"Briney's fine, Rosie," he said. "He's doing a good job at the mill. We're all grateful to him for stepping in like the man that he is going to be."

Well, there was nothing I could say after that, was there, except to ask Mister O'Grady to send my good wishes to Briney. I couldn't help adding that maybe, perhaps, Briney might find the time to come by and let me know how he was doing himself?

At that, Mister O'Grady laughed and said he was sure Briney would be doing that as soon as he could.

I must admit I blushed and then felt so foolish I had to hide myself back in the house while Kevin fetched in the water.

Wednesday, May 22nd, 1867

After dinner this evening, Mister Bradley called us all in, even Cook and James and Fanny, and told us a bit more about what is going to happen. He said that we should all know what momentous happenings are going on. I did particularly like that word *momentous*. It sounds so important. And, indeed, what is going on is important. Here is what he said. I paid strict attention and memorized his words as he said them.

Mister Macdonald did bring back the British North America Act that gives us a constitution and makes us a country instead of a collection of British colonies. We will still owe allegiance to the Queen, of course. She has chosen her representative in British North America, Lord Monck, who was governor general of the Province of Canada, to be governor general of the new country. He has appointed Mister Macdonald to be the country's first prime minister.

With the birth of the **Dominion of Canada** (the governor general's very words — the **Dominion of Canada** — I am writing them big and bold), the two parts of the Province of Canada, Canada East and Canada West, will become two separate provinces, known as Québec and Ontario. We will be in Ontario, Mam and Da will be in Québec. The Provinces of New Brunswick and Nova Scotia will be included in the new country, and Mister Bradley says it is only a matter of time before Prince Edward Island joins in. What a proud thing that will be!

He is not so certain about Newfoundland, though, and as he said before, the colony of British Columbia is much too far away to be included.

All this will come into being formally on July 1st, and there is to be a grand celebration on that day. Now that it is actually happening, and I have no more worries about losing my family, I can hardly wait!

Thursday, May 23rd, 1867

I planted Mary Margaret's lobelia seedlings today beside the front doorway. Cook and I started planting the kitchen garden as well. The weather has been fine, with just enough rain to encourage everything to grow. If we can keep that clumsy dog from trampling the plants, of course.

Saturday, May 25th, 1867

Briney came round today and we walked down to the canal to watch the boats locking through. The first thing I did was apologize for being so hard on him for working at the mill. I told him I now understood better that he has to do it.

He told me that Thomas is not doing well at all. His leg was crushed as well as broken, and the doctor does not hold out much hope that he will ever be able to walk properly again. That means that Briney definitely will be working at the mill permanently. I almost burst out with a protest to that, but managed to shut my mouth firmly and hold my tongue.

We have to do what we have to do, and it's not always to our liking.

Mister Jim Fleming is the lockmaster at the canal, and he came over to talk to us when he saw us watching the boats. He and his family live in a very nice house up at Chaffey's Lock and he makes the rounds checking the other locks every day. He talked to us for ages, telling us all about the history of the canal, until a boat horn sounded and he had to go and lock the boat through.

I never knew that so many people died during the building of the canal. Conditions were even worse then than they are today — hard to imagine, but true. And, as well, there was an outbreak of a disease called malaria that killed hundreds of people. It must have been dreadful.

Mister Fleming told us that the locks aren't as busy as they used to be, because of all the new canals on the St. Lawrence River, but it still looked busy to me. While we were there we saw tugs towing two or three barges — one tug was even towing four barges. There were several sailing scows that Mister Fleming told us were carrying all sorts of goods and foodstuffs. They used to bring the big lumber rafts through here too, Mister Fleming said, although we did not see any today.

What we did see was a huge passenger steamer which was as big as the steamer we took to Cacouna. It was coming up from Kingston to Ottawa. It had a lovely musical steam whistle that I'm sure could be heard for miles. The decks were crowded with people, all waving and laughing. I waved back, although Briney was too shy to do so. It was amazing to see it so close up there beside us. I could have reached out and touched the people on the deck as Mister Fleming let the water out of the lock and the boat went down.

All in all, we spent the entire afternoon there. I have not enjoyed a day so much in a long time.

Monday, May 27th, 1867

Mister Bradley said something tonight that got me thinking about a matter that I've never thought of before. He was annoyed because the Indians are requesting compensation for the land that was taken from them and given to European settlers. Mister Bradley thinks they should be satisfied with the land they were given for a reserve at Maniwaki on the Gatineau River.

Did they once really own all this land? Seems to me that if they did, a reserve would hardly make up for losing it. I asked if they were paid anything for it and Mister Bradley looked at me as if I were daft.

"Of course not," he said. "They didn't really own the land. They just lived here."

Thursday, May 30th, 1867

Missus Bradley went shopping today and took me along to carry her purchases, as usual. She wanted to buy a new hat, among other things.

We went to a store where they sold hats and I wondered how Missus Bradley would ever be able to choose. There were hats of every description there, beribboned, festooned with silk flowers, some with wide brims, some with narrow brims, straw, felt . . . I could write pages of descriptions of them all.

Missus Bradley tried on at least ten. She was having as lovely a time choosing as I was watching. Finally she made her decision, and I think she chose the most beautiful hat of all. It has a narrow, grey felt brim, and is piled high on top with a profusion of lilac flowers and soft green leaves, all made of silk. When she tried it on, it fair took my breath away, it did.

Then she decided she must have a new scarf to go with it. Clouds, the ladies here call their scarves, and clouds they look like. She chose a silvery grey one made of the lightest possible wool. It just drifted around her shoulders and matched the hat wonderfully. I was laden down with packages by the time we started for home.

Friday, May 31ˢᵗ, 1867

The weather is so fine, Mister and Missus Bradley are planning a picnic up into the Chelsea Hills tomorrow. Fanny is not well, so I am to go to take care of baby Jonathan. Needless to say, I am happy about that, although sorry that Fanny is ill. She is right miserable. Not even Fanny deserves to feel that horrible.

Cook is busy preparing a huge hamper of food and we shall not starve.

Saturday, June 1st, 1867

The picnic was delightful, but the day most certainly did not go as planned, and I have the bumps and bruises to show for it.

Mister Bradley had arranged to meet up with Mister and Missus Forrester, and to my delight they brought Bessie with them to help out. They had their own horse and trap and followed along behind us.

Missus Bradley wished to drive the horse and Mister Bradley sat up beside her, beaming. He is so proud of her driving ability.

She looked grand with her new hat and her lovely cloud billowing around her shoulders in the wind. Bessie told me later that Mister Forrester thought it a bit of a scandal that Missus Bradley drove. He thought she drove too fast. I did not, but in light of what happened, I am sure he thinks he was right.

I sat in the back of the trap with Jonathan in my arms. He's a happy baby and so bright. He was looking at everything and I could tell he was taking it all in. All smiles he was too. I think he was as happy to be with me as I was with him.

We drove up into the hills and found a spot to lay out the blankets where we could look down over the valley to the Ottawa River winding below. There was a bit of a breeze to help drive off those horrible little biting black flies, but we still kept baby Jonathan well covered. Cook had given us cat-mint oil to rub on our hands and necks. It helped a bit to repel the insects, but I must wash it off before I see Sophie and her kittens. It will drive them wild.

The kittens are almost old enough to go to their new homes now. I have found homes for them all, but they are so sweet and such fun to have around, I shall miss them.

The trees are all out in leaf now and there was a soft green bloom to the whole scene. I've never seen a lovelier sight. Cook had made a feast. Missus Bradley took Jonathan while I unpacked the hampers and laid it out.

There were slices of cooked ham and fresh bread, still warm. Some roasted chicken and a poultry pie. As if that weren't enough, Missus Forrester brought several packets of dainty sandwiches such as are usually served for tea. She also brought tarts for dessert and coconut patties — favourites of mine, but hard to come by because of the coconut. Missus Forrester had bought a packet of it when she was in Québec. Our Cook had made Victoria cakes and molasses cookies. (I like the Victoria cakes, and even helped make them, but I am not too fond of molasses. I would put the recipe down for the Victoria cakes, but I'm too tired to remember it. They are good, though, and I have one sitting here by my bed as I write.)

Missus Forrester brought raspberry vinegar mixed with water to drink.

Cook had also packed a small kerosene burner so that we could boil water for tea. Bessie and I were sent to find a spring to fill the kettle and it did not take us long to do so. The water poured out of a crack in the hillside and was so fresh and cold we drank our fill of it as well as filling the kettle.

Bessie and I were allowed to choose what we wanted from the lovely assortment of good things to eat, then we took the baby and went over to sit under a tree out of the sun, to eat until it was time to clear up.

It was all as grand as could be . . . but then we headed back home.

All was going well until we got near the bottom of the hill. At that point a whole pack of dogs suddenly raced out of the bush and startled our horse. The horse panicked and bolted. Missus Bradley is a good driver, but even so she lost control for a moment. Before she could get the horse back under control, one wheel slipped off the path into the ditch. It was the wheel on the side where I was sitting holding baby Jonathan.

The wheel broke. The whole trap tilted and

before I knew what was happening, the babe and I were thrown out.

All I could think of was to hold the babe tight and not let go of him, so I could not put out a hand to break my fall. I fell hard into the ditch, but fortunately on my side, and rolled onto my back, still holding tight to Jonathan. I came to rest facing up to the sky. For a moment I just lay there, staring at the clouds and wondering what had happened and where I was. I vaguely remember Missus Bradley screaming.

The next thing I remember is Mister Bradley leaning over me and taking the babe from my arms. Jonathan was not even crying. So wrapped up he was, I don't think he even felt a bump, and didn't he just give me the biggest smile ever.

Mister Bradley gave the babe to Missus Bradley, who leaped off the pony trap to see to him, then he helped me up. I was in a right state. The Forresters stopped behind us and Mister Forrester drove the dogs off with his horse whip. Missus Forrester and Bessie helped me into their cart and sat me down. Everyone made such a fuss over me, I was more embarrassed by all the attention than hurt. Mister Bradley stayed with our cart, while the Forresters drove Missus Bradley, baby Jonathan and me back home.

I am being hailed as a hero again and made much of. Missus Bradley was in a flurry and full of apologies, as if the accident had been her fault, which it certainly was not. In any case, she insisted that I take to my bed as soon as we got home. She had Cook bring me hot soup and a few Victoria cakes, but I was still so upset that I could not face the thought of soup or any other food.

I do not think I did anything heroic. I just hung on to Jonathan, but I do ache in just about every bone of my body.

I might just manage one Victoria cake now, though.

Monday, June 3ʳᵈ, 1867

Fanny is so ill that Missus Bradley has allowed her to go home to her mother. That means that I am nursemaid again. I'm delighted about that, as I love that wee baby so.

Thursday, June 6ᵗʰ, 1867

Something dreadful has happened.

I was called into the parlour this morning to find both Mister and Missus Bradley there. They were looking very grim.

"We have a problem, Rosie," Mister Bradley said. "A very valuable bracelet of Missus Bradley's has gone missing."

My heart sank down to my boots. Surely they were not accusing me of taking it!

They weren't, not in so many words, but I was

sure that there was a certain amount of suspicion. I hotly denied knowing anything about it and, I'm embarrassed to say, I burst into tears. Missus Bradley was quick to comfort me, but there was a certain restraint to her words. She and Mister Bradley have been so kind to me. Now I'm afraid that this has cast a shadow over everything. They certainly didn't seem the same as usual.

They let me go, finally, and I escaped to the kitchen, only to find James and Cook sitting at the table. James was quick to look me up and down with a sneer.

"You'd better come clean, my girl," he said. "That was a costly bracelet. They'll find you out if you took it, you can be sure of that."

I cried even harder, but didn't Cook get up and put her arm around me.

"Leave the girl alone," she said. "If Rosie says she didn't take it, then she didn't. I know if a girl is a liar and a thief or not, and Rosie certainly is not."

James just lifted an eyebrow and sauntered out of the room.

Monday, June 10th, 1867

I have not been accused of the theft, but the bracelet has not been found.

❧

Wednesday, June 12th, 1867

Nothing more is being said about the bracelet, but there is an uncomfortable feeling between Missus Bradley and myself that did not exist before.

James cannot look at me without a knowing sneer on his face.

I do not know how long I can stand this.

Friday, June 14th, 1867

There is talk of nothing now but the celebration on the 1st of July, when we will be officially proclaimed the Dominion of Canada. But I am so upset about the missing bracelet that I cannot bring myself to be much interested in it at all anymore.

Saturday, June 15th, 1867

News came today that poor Fanny has died from the influenza. Missus Bradley is so upset that the business of the bracelet seems to have been forgotten.

It has not been forgotten by me, however. I feel there is a shadow hanging over me and I am sick about it. And it most certainly has not been forgotten by James. He takes every opportunity to make it clear that he, at least, believes me to be a thief.

A nasty thought has crept into my head. What if Fanny stole the bracelet and now she is dead? No one will ever know the truth of it.

Oh, I cannot bear this — I have to get away from here!

I haven't sent my wages home for this month yet . . .

I've decided that I'm going to bundle my few possessions up right now and slip out early tomorrow morning before anyone is up. I will buy a train ticket and be out of here and home within three days.

There's nothing else to be done.

Sunday, June 16th, 1867

I did not go.

I was ready to go as soon as everyone else had left for church. I even got as far as the door. Then I stopped.

I thought about Mam and Da's faces when I walked in. What would they think of me, running away like that? What kind of an example would I set for the little ones? And what would Mary Margaret think? She would be disappointed to death with me.

I stuffed my things back in the little chest in my room where I keep them, and sank back down onto my bed. I could not help weeping, but I did not go.

Still, I am heartsick. To think that I must live in a house where I am suspected of being a thief!

Monday, June 24th, 1867

Life goes on. Da always used to say that, but I never knew the truth of it until now. I know I have done the right thing by staying and not running away. Somehow or other I have to get through this, but it is hard.

Tuesday, June 25th, 1867

I told Briney today about what happened. I didn't mean to tell him about almost running away, but that came out too. I was astonished at how angry he got.

First of all, he was furious that anyone suspected me of stealing.

"How could anyone think that!" he cried. I think he would have charged into the parlour and taken the Bradleys to task that very moment if I hadn't grabbed onto him.

Then he was furious with me for even thinking of leaving.

"What of me?" he demanded. "Did you not think of how I would feel if you had gone?"

I was so stunned by that, I couldn't answer. Would it really have mattered that much to him?

Then I began to think about how I would have felt when I had come to my senses and realized what I had done — and I haven't stopped thinking about it since.

Wednesday, June 26th, 1867

The dog has done something good. I took baby Jonathan out in his perambulator today for a walk.

Went all the way to the canal and watched the boats for a while, then started back. The weather was lovely and warm and he was enjoying the fresh air. It's a blessing to get away from the putrid air in this house and must be good for him. I could almost enjoy it too.

We were nearly home when I suddenly saw, to my horror, Daisy's friend the cow, with two of her friends, heading into our front garden. I had forgotten to close the gate!

I could only imagine the trouble I would be in if those lumbering beasts trampled the flowers and bushes of Missus Bradley's front garden that have taken so long to establish.

I started to run, pushing the perambulator — a little perilously, I must admit — ahead of me. Baby Jonathan seemed to like the bumpy speed, though. He gurgled and crowed quite happily. Just as I got up to the house and the reality of how I was going to herd those cows out of the garden was beginning to sink in, and my heart was about to sink accordingly, who should erupt from the backyard but Brutus.

He fairly tore at those animals. I had no idea he could bark so loudly, nor growl so fiercely. Even knowing him as I do, I was taken aback. He charged the cows, and the cows stopped dead in their tracks, then beat a hasty retreat. Hasty for cows, that is, which isn't really all that hasty.

Brutus has certainly saved the garden and, more importantly, me. I can hardly bring myself to be grateful, but grateful I must be.

I will give him a biscuit tonight when nobody is watching.

I still can't abide the beast, but perhaps I will have to try to have a more charitable opinion of him.

Thursday, June 27*th*, 1867

A new nursemaid came today. Her name is Elsie. Right different from Fanny she is. I will not speak ill of the dead, but I think Elsie will be a deal easier to get along with. Only now I have to give Jonathan up again.

Fanny. Every time I think of her, I wonder if it was she who took that bracelet. It must have been. Who else could have done it? If she did, we will never know the truth of it and I will be suspected of being a thief for as long as I live.

But there, I'm suspecting *her* with no proof, and that's just as mean as it is for anyone to suspect me with no proof.

Friday, June 28*th*, 1867

I am to have the 1*st* of July off. Bessie has arranged to meet with me to go and see the ceremonies on Parliament Hill. Briney is to get the day off too, and Jean-Louis came around to say he will meet up with us as well. It would be such a merry day if I were not still so sick about the bracelet. I have searched every inch of this house over and over, hoping to find it, but no luck.

Saturday, June 29th, 1867

Mister Bradley had a grand surprise for Missus Bradley today. He has bought a lot on Daly Street in Sandy Hill, not far from Mister Besserer's house at number 149. They will start construction on a new home next week, and Mister Bradley says they will be able to move in before next winter. He says he will not have his wife go through another winter in this drafty, smelly little house. A fine big stone house, it will be.

I wonder if they will want me to move there with them. They might not, because of this accursed business of the bracelet.

What will I do then?

Sunday, June 30th, 1867

Tomorrow is the big day.

It is very late now, but I just had to write this down. At midnight, the bells of all the churches in Ottawa were let loose and began to peal. We all of us went outside to stand in the street and listen. It was surely magnificent, but all it did was make me weep.

Monday, July 1st, 1867
Ottawa, The Dominion of Canada

Where to start? It is very late and everyone in the house is finally asleep. I did not sleep last night, and I am certain I will not sleep tonight either.

It was a hot, sunny day. Just perfect for all the festivities. Mister Bradley was off early to the Parliament Buildings, as he said that Lord Monck, the governor general, was to swear in the new Cabinet. He told us that the governor general has also announced that Mister Macdonald has been made a Knight Commander of the Bath by order of Queen Victoria. He will now be **Sir John A. Macdonald**. I am writing those words big and bold too.

As soon as I had helped Cook tidy up the kitchen after our breakfast, I was off. Bessie was waiting for me by the Rideau Bridge and we found Jean-Louis up on Parliament Hill. I was happy to see Briney was there with him.

I have never seen such a sight as the multitude of people and carriages that crowded Parliament Hill. There was not one clear space. We managed to squirm our way through so that we could get close to the Parliament Buildings to watch the parade and the military review, and very impressive it was. The band music was so lively it was impossible not to tap your feet in time to it. For a while I was even able to forget my worries and allow myself to enjoy the festivities a little bit.

There was an incident that Mister Bradley declared was a "deplorable accident," but that Briney and I thought was the highlight of the morning. The Civil Service Rifle Company lined up on both sides of Sparks Street to fire a hundred-and-one-gun salute. We all waited breathlessly for it, but they forgot to remove their ramrods from their rifles. Along with the great noise of the shots, all the ramrods sailed away up in the air over our heads! People dodged and screamed, but we just stood with our mouths open and laughed. It was a good addition to the celebrations, I thought.

There was a picnic this afternoon for the parishioners and their children from St. Alban's, in New Edinburgh. Missus Bradley was keen to go and, as Elsie had the day off, I went as well to care for baby Jonathan. We took the pony trap, but there was no talk of Missus Bradley driving today and Mister Bradley took the reins. I think Missus Bradley handles the horse better.

As usual, Cook had packed a great hamper full of food and we settled down beneath a tree to watch all the festivities. Everyone but me was in a grand mood. There were speeches, and races, and children were allowed to run around like little wild things.

Some of the adults got quite carried away and the Reverend Dr. Thomas Bedford-Jones forgot his dignity completely and ended up in a piggyback race with a local judge. If I hadn't been so despondent, I'm sure I would have found it funny.

We stayed there until suppertime, then, seeing that Missus Bradley was tiring, Mister Bradley drove us home. The celebrations were not over, however, as there was to be a grand display of fireworks after sunset.

Briney turned up after supper to beg permission from Mister Bradley for me to go see the fireworks with him. Mister Bradley was a little hesitant, but it was such a special day, he finally relented and agreed that I could go. I have never seen anything like that display. The colours were fair dazzling. I think their images are still etched into my brain, and the sounds of them taking off and exploding high above us are still echoing in my ears.

As we were walking home, I was so bedazzled that I didn't even realize that Briney had taken hold of my hand! It wasn't until we reached the doorstep of the Bradleys' house that I came to my senses and snatched it away.

And then didn't the daft boy say, "I'm glad you didn't leave. I'm right fond of you, Rosie Dunn."

Well, thanks be it was dark enough that he couldn't see the blush that must have turned my face scarlet.

"Get on with you, you foolish boy," I said, with as much dignity as I could muster. I'm afraid it wasn't much, though.

Briney just laughed and tipped his cap to me and went off down the street whistling like a lunatic.

There are still bonfires in the streets and I can hear sounds of celebrations all over the town.

So it is done. In spite of all the talk and confusion and opposition, we are now a country of our own.

Happy Birthday, Canada.

Wednesday, July 3rd, 1867

Now that all the fuss and celebration of Confederation is over, Mister and Missus Bradley are making plans for the new house in earnest.

There has been no mention of me going with them. I cannot help but think that the matter of that lost bracelet is still hovering over me. Perhaps I should have left after all.

But no, no matter what happens now, I couldn't have.

Thursday, July 4th, 1867

Missus Bradley called me into the parlour today. Mister Bradley was there with her and they both looked so serious, I suddenly felt sick.

Here it is, then, I thought. They're going to tell me they don't want me in the new house with them. Perhaps they've already hired a girl to replace me. I braced myself for the worst, but that's not what happened.

Missus Bradley spoke first. "It's about that wretched missing bracelet of mine," she said. "Cook tells me you are still upset about it. That you feel as if you are under suspicion."

I couldn't speak. I could only manage a small kind of a nod.

"Oh, Rosie, I'm so sorry!" she said. "I was distressed when I discovered it missing, but Mister Bradley and I want you to know that we don't for a moment think that you took it. We know you would never steal from us."

"You mean you want me to stay?" I blurted out. "You do want me to come with you to the new house?" I must confess I burst into tears of relief.

"Of course we do!" Missus Bradley said. She put her arm around me. "Why would you ever think that we wouldn't?"

Mister Bradley patted me on the shoulder.

"You're part of the family now, Rosie," he said, and I have never heard him speak more kindly. "We couldn't imagine getting along without you."

Part of the family.

As I sit here writing this, all snug in my bed with Sophie purring beside me, muddy old Ottawa seems like not such a bad place after all. In fact, it feels as if this is exactly where I was meant to be.

It seems that I, too, have moved on.

I cannot wait to see Briney and tell him.

Epilogue

Rosie and Briney were married when Rosie turned eighteen. By then Briney had a good, permanent job with the E.B. Eddy sawmill, and when that mill was converted into the E.B. Eddy Manufacturing Company to produce matches and other items made of wood, several years later, Briney was promoted to a foreman's position. Because of this, and by working with Missus Bradley from time to time for some extra money, Rosie was able to ensure that all six of their children finished secondary education.

Two of their boys followed their father into the mill and did as well as he had. Two other boys left Ottawa to seek their fortunes elsewhere. One signed on to a steamer and travelled regularly to England and Europe. He never failed to bring back souvenirs from his travels. Rosie particularly delighted in anything Irish that he could find for her.

The other son went on Rosie's detested train cars and became an engineer. Despite her son's fascination with the railway, Rosie never did come to like travel by rail.

One of her daughters took secretarial training and was employed on Parliament Hill as a secretary to a member of parliament. The other daughter became a teacher.

Rosie was immensely proud of the fact that

none of their children had to go into service.

Unfortunately, Briney's brother Thomas was never able to return to work at the mill, though he was able to find odd jobs in the town. After his parents died, he came to live with Rosie and Briney and became a beloved uncle to their children.

Bessie and Rosie remained friends for all of their lives, although Bessie continued to irritate Rosie once in a while with her "high-falutin'" ways. She married a man who worked in the mill as well. She and her husband had five children, but Bessie was widowed when her husband was killed in a mill accident. Rosie and Briney helped her out considerably during the hard times that followed that accident.

Shy Jean-Louis, to everyone's surprise, became a well-respected politician. He married a young woman who was very active in the cause of French rights. He and Briney remained friends as well, and his wife became a friend of Rosie's, although they sometimes had their differences — as did all the French and Irish in Ottawa at that time. Both Rosie and Marie could get somewhat vehement in their discussions, which worried both husbands, but that didn't damage their friendship. In fact, Rosie's eldest son married Jean-Louis and Marie's eldest daughter. That made for lively conversations around the dinner table.

One of the highlights of Rosie's life was when

their children pooled their resources and sent Rosie and Briney on a trip to Ireland. Although their parents had died by then, Rosie and Briney were able to visit the villages from which their parents had come when *they* were young, and meet many long-lost relatives. Rosie loved Ireland, but Ottawa was home to her by then and she was glad to return to Canada when their visit was done.

Briney and Rosie lived to a good old age. Briney teased Rosie to the end, always threatening to buy a cow and name it Rosie, but he never did. Rosie said he wouldn't dare, and she was probably right.

And that bracelet?

Nothing more was said about it, but when James was cleaning out the pony trap later in the summer of 1867, he found it wedged down beside the front seat. The Bradleys determined that it must have fallen off when they had their accident. It gave Rosie great pleasure to hear James have to admit that he had judged her unfairly, and she was able to put her own suspicions of poor Fanny to rest.

Historical Note

The road to Confederation and to the creation of the Dominion of Canada was a long one. British North America at that time was composed of the Province of British Columbia far in the west; the Province of Canada; and the Provinces of Prince Edward Island, Nova Scotia, New Brunswick and Newfoundland in the east. Between them was Rupert's Land.

The Province of Canada had been formed in 1841 by uniting Canada West (formerly Upper Canada) and Canada East (formerly Lower Canada). Canada West was mainly English-speaking and Protestant, and Canada East was mainly French-speaking and Roman Catholic, with a substantial English Protestant minority. By the 1860s, however, the two parts of the Province of Canada had come to a political deadlock. One of the many problems they could not agree on was a mutually beneficial economic policy.

The deadlock between Canada West and Canada East gave rise to the idea of forming a larger British North American union. Britain's colonies on the Atlantic were already talking about creating their own regional union.

The co-premier of the Province of Canada was John A. Macdonald. He had led his Liberal-Conservative Party into a Great Coalition with the Parti bleu of George-Étienne Cartier and George Brown's Clear Grits. Together, with a view to forming this larger British North American Union, the three leaders asked if the Province of Canada could be included in the negotiations.

The Atlantic provinces had already set the date for a conference discussing *their* union, in Charlottetown, Prince Edward Island — September 1, 1864. Macdonald, Cartier and Brown were invited, and presented their proposal for a united government of all the provinces, with the preservation of ties with Great Britain. By September 7, 1864, the delegates from Nova Scotia, New Brunswick and Prince Edward Island gave a positive answer to the Canadian delegation. Delegates from the three Maritime provinces and Newfoundland were then invited to attend another conference held in Québec City in October of 1864.

There were many differences to be hammered out at this conference, but most were finally resolved, and the delegates came up with seventy-two resolutions. Following this last conference, the Province of Canada's legislature passed a bill approving the union. New Brunswick and Nova Scotia harboured reservations about the union, however, and did not opt in until 1866. Prince Edward Island and Newfoundland decided not to join.

In November 1866, sixteen delegates from the

Province of Canada, New Brunswick and Nova Scotia travelled to London, England. They were granted an audience with Queen Victoria, and subsequently passed their seventy-two resolutions, which then became known as the London Resolution. Amendments that the Nova Scotians had wished included did not pass, however, and this led to more misgivings on their part.

In January 1867, the delegates drafted the British North America Act. It was decided that the new country should be called Canada, but there was considerable debate about how it should be designated. Kingdom and Confederation, among other options, were ultimately rejected, and the term Dominion was finally decided upon. Canada West would enter Confederation as Ontario, and Canada East would enter as Québec. After the presentation of the Act to Queen Victoria on February 11, 1867, the bill was introduced in the House of Lords the next day. It was approved first by them, then by the British House of Commons. It received the Queen's assent on March 29, 1867. July 1, 1867, was decided upon as the date for the union.

Although there was, and continued to be, disagreement and dissatisfaction among some parties in Canada about the union, it seemed that there was no such concern in Great Britain. Indeed, it was suggested, perhaps tongue in cheek, that Great Britain was in favour of it because if the colonies united into one country and the United States ever invaded again, they could defend themselves without Great Britain having to get involved.

Rupert's Land — the huge tract of land situated between British Columbia and the eastern provinces of Canada — was owned by the Hudson's Bay Company. The HBC transferred Rupert's Land to the Government of Canada in June 1870; along with the North-Western Territory, it became the North-West Territories. A small part of this territory became the Province of Manitoba when it joined Confederation on July 15, 1870. The North-West Territories remained virtually a crown colony of Canada.

British Columbia joined Confederation on July 20, 1871.

Prince Edward Island joined on July 1, 1873.

A part of the North-West Territories was separated off on June 13, 1898, to become the Yukon Territory. It is currently known as Yukon.

Saskatchewan and Alberta, also formerly part of the North-West Territories, joined on September 1, 1905.

In 1912, the Parliament of Canada made the official name of these territories the Northwest Territories, dropping all hyphenated forms of the name.

Newfoundland joined on March 31, 1949. It was renamed Newfoundland and Labrador in 2001.

The British North America Act, which gave Canada its constitution as well as the power to amend that constitution, remained an Act of the Parliament of Great Britain. Then, in 1982, Prime Minister Pierre Elliott Trudeau brought the British North America Act home to Canada. It was renamed the Constitution Act, 1867, and became part of the new constitution of Canada.

Nunavut Territory was separated officially from the Northwest Territories on April 1, 1999.

The Parliament Buildings were begun in 1859, and mostly completed by the time of Confederation. The Peace Tower was not finished until 1927; it was named to commemorate the end of the First World War.

Animals such as pigs and cows roamed freely, even on Sparks Street, now one of Ottawa's best-known streets.

In this 1867 photograph, the elegant Parliament Buildings in the background contrast with the rougher buildings of the remote lumber town.

Ottawa was notoriously muddy. Many streets had no sidewalks, or very narrow ones, and water drained along open channels in the roads.

Built between 1826 and 1832, the Rideau Canal's locks allowed ships to reach Ottawa from Lake Ontario at Kingston, and avoid the rapids at the Rideau and Cataraqui rivers.

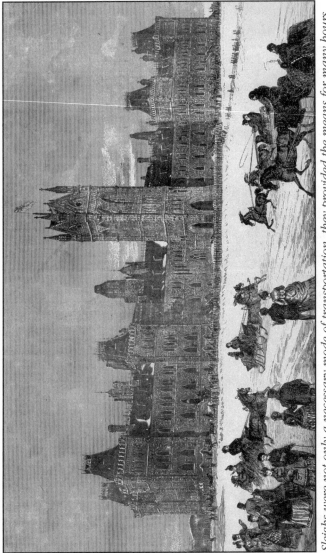

Sleighs were not only a necessary mode of transportation, they provided the means for many hours of pleasure and enjoyment.

Timber chutes called "sliders" allowed lumber rafts to bypass the rapids, then continue to the many mills downstream.

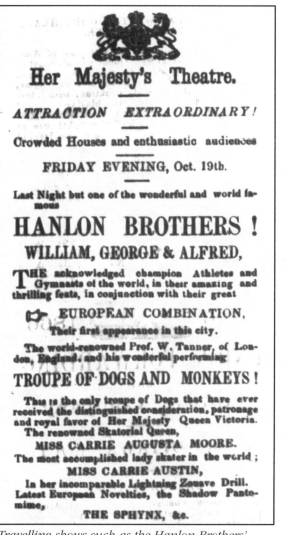

Travelling shows such as the Hanlon Brothers' Circus, as well as P.T. Barnum's Great Travelling Museum, promised "the most stupendous array of talent ever congregated in one entertainment."

Montreal. Steamer in Lachine Rapids.

Even paddlewheel steamers, such as the Corsican in this vintage postcard, braved the fierce Lachine Rapids south of Montreal.

The fashionable resort of Cacouna drew many civil servants' families in the summer months. Bathers were dressed from neck to ankle.

(Upper) John A. Macdonald of the Liberal-Conservatives and Thomas D'Arcy McGee (lower) joined with George-Étienne Cartier of the Parti blue and George Brown of the Clear Grits to become driving forces behind Confederation.

BY THE QUEEN.

A PROCLAMATION

For Uniting the Provinces of Canada, Nova Scotia, and New Brunswick into One Dominion under the Name of CANADA.

VICTORIA R.

WHEREAS by an Act of Parliament passed on the Twenty-ninth Day of March One thousand eight hundred and sixty-seven, in the Thirtieth Year of Our Reign, intituled "An Act for the Union of Canada, Nova Scotia, and New Brunswick, and the "Government thereof, and for Purposes connected therewith," after divers Recitals, it is enacted, that "It shall be lawful for the Queen, by and with the Advice of Her Majesty's most Honorable "Privy Council, to declare by Proclamation that on and after a Day therein appointed, not being "more than Six Months after the passing of this Act, the Provinces of Canada, Nova Scotia, and "New Brunswick shall form and be One Dominion under the Name of Canada, and on and after "that Day those Three Provinces shall form and be One Dominion under that Name accordingly:" And it is thereby further enacted, that "such Persons shall be first summoned to the Senate as "the Queen, by Warrant under Her Majesty's Royal Sign Manual, thinks fit to approve, and "their Names shall be inserted in the Queen's Proclamation of Union:" We therefore, by and with the Advice of Our Privy Council, have thought fit to issue this Our Royal Proclamation, and We do Ordain, Declare, and Command, that on and after the First Day of July One thousand eight hundred and sixty-seven the Provinces of Canada, Nova Scotia, and New Brunswick shall form and be One Dominion under the Name of Canada. And We do further Ordain and Declare, that the Persons whose Names are herein inserted and set forth are the Persons of whom We have, by Warrant under Our Royal Sign Manual, thought fit to approve as the Persons who shall be first summoned to the Senate of Canada.

FOR THE PROVINCE OF ONTARIO.	FOR THE PROVINCE OF QUEBEC.	FOR THE PROVINCE OF NOVA SCOTIA.	FOR THE PROVINCE OF NEW BRUNSWICK.
JOHN HAMILTON,	JAMES LESLIE,	EDWARD KENNY,	AMOS EDWIN BOTSFORD,
RODERICK MATHESON,	ASA BELKNAP FOSTER,	JONATHAN M'CULLY,	EDWARD BARRON CHANDLER,
JOHN ROSS,	JOSEPH NOËL BOSSÉ,	THOMAS D. ARCHIBALD,	JOHN ROBERTSON,
SAMUEL MILLS,	LOUIS A. OLIVIER,	ROBERT B. DICKEY,	ROBERT LEONARD HAZEN,
BENJAMIN SEYMOUR,	JACQUE OLIVIER BUREAU,	JOHN H. ANDERSON,	WILLIAM HUNTER ODELL,
WALTER HAMILTON DICKSON,	CHARLES MALHIOT,	JOHN HOLMES,	DAVID WARK,
JAMES SHAW,	LOUIS RENAUD,	JOHN W. RITCHIE,	WILLIAM HENRY STEEVES,
ADAM JOHNSTON FERGUSON BLAIR,	LUC LETELLIER DE ST. JUST,	BENJAMIN WIER,	WILLIAM TODD,
ALEXANDER CAMPBELL,	ULRIC JOSEPH TESSIER,	JOHN LOCKE,	JOHN FERGUSON,
DAVID CHRISTIE,	JOHN HAMILTON,	CALEB R. BILL,	ROBERT DUNCAN WILMOT,
JAMES COX AIKINS,	CHARLES CORMIER,	JOHN BOURINOT,	ABNER REID M'CLELAN,
DAVID REESOR,	ANTOINE JUCHEREAU DUCHESNAY,	WILLIAM MILLER.	PETER MITCHELL.
ELIJAH LEONARD,	DAVID EDWARD PRICE,		
WILLIAM MACMASTER,	ELZEAR H. J. DUCHESNAY,		
ASA ALLWORTH BURNHAM,	LEANDRE DUMOUCHEL,		
JOHN SIMPSON,	LOUIS LACOSTE,		
JAMES SKEAD,	JOSEPH F. ARMAND,		
DAVID LEWIS MACPHERSON,	CHARLES WILSON,		
GEORGE CRAWFORD,	WILLIAM HENRY CHAFFERS,		
DONALD MACDONALD,	JEAN BAPTISTE GUÉVREMONT,		
OLIVER BLAKE,	JAMES FERRIER,		
BILLA FLINT,	Sir NARCISSE FORTUNAT BELLEAU, Knight,		
WALTER M'CREA,	THOMAS RYAN,		
GEORGE WILLIAM ALLAN.	JOHN SEWELL SANBORN.		

Queen Victoria's royal proclamation of March 29th, 1867, decreed that " . . . the Provinces of Canada, Nova Scotia, and New Brunswick shall form and be One Dominion under the Name of Canada."

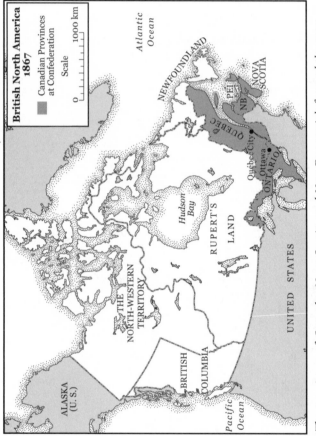

Atlantic Ocean

NEWFOUNDLAND

PEI

NB

NOVA SCOTIA

QUEBEC

Quebec City

Ottawa

ONTARIO

Hudson Bay

RUPERT'S LAND

THE NORTH-WESTERN TERRITORY

UNITED STATES

BRITISH COLUMBIA

ALASKA (U. S.)

Pacific Ocean

The provinces of Canada, Nova Scotia and New Brunswick formed the new Dominion of Canada in 1867. Prince Edward Island, Newfoundland, portions of Rupert's Land, and British Columbia did not join until later.

Acknowledgements

❦

Cover cameo (detail): *A Village Maiden, 1886,* Sir George Clausen, Bridgeman Art Library International, CH 497785.
Cover background (detail): Parliament Building, Centre Block, Library and Archives Canada, C-002255.

Page 166: Centre Block, Parliament Buildings under construction, Samuel McLaughlin, Library and Archives Canada, C-003039.
Page 167: Sparks St. West end Corner of Kent Street, Harry Walker, Library and Archives Canada, C-011384.
Page 168: Looking West from Court House to Parliament Hill, Acc. No. 1976-33-1, Samuel McLaughlin, Library and Archives Canada, C-001185.
Page 169: Horse-drawn omnibus on Sparks. St. between Elgin and Metcalfe St., City of Ottawa Archives, CA-001504.
Page 170: Locks on the Rideau Canal, Ottawa, ON, about 1890; Topley Studio, Gift of Mr. Stanley G. Triggs, © McCord Museum, MP-0000.25.163.
Page 171: Front View of the Parliament Building, Library and Archives Canada, Acc. No. 1976-33-1, Gift from Ralph Greenhill, C-048710.
Page 172: Timber slide, Ottawa, ON, 1866, William Notman, © McCord Museum, 1-22716.1.
Page 173: Hanlon Brothers' ad, *Ottawa Citizen,* October 29, 1866.
Page 174: *Montreal. Steamer* Corsican *in the Great Lakes,* from a Notman photograph, courtesy of Walter Lewis, from Maritime History of the Great Lakes website.
Page 175: At the Beach, Collections Canada, C-023503.
Page 176 (left): Sir John A. Macdonald, K.C.B, WIlliam Notman, National Archives of Canada, C-030440.
Page 176 (right): Portrait of Thomas D'Arcy McGee, William Notman, Library and Archives Canada, C-016749.
Page 177: The Royal Proclamation of March 29, 1867, National Archives of Canada, C-060281.
Page 178: Map by Paul Heersink/Paperglyphs.

The publisher wishes to thank Barbara Hehner for her attention to the factual details, and Dr. Ross Fair of Ryerson University for sharing his historical expertise.

For my family,
each and every one of them

Author's Note

♦

In the mid-1980s, on a trip to England to research the book I was writing, I struck up a conversation with the woman sitting next to me on the plane. She was Sandra Gwyn, returning to London after a book tour in Canada, promoting her history of Ottawa, *The Private Capital*. Little did I know then how invaluable this excellent book would be to me over twenty years later, when I was writing my own book about Ottawa at the time of Confederation. I am deeply indebted to her and her book, with its detailed descriptions of muddy Ottawa in its early years.

Along with Rosie, I could most particularly identify with the smells Sandra Gwyn described. My husband and I moved to Ottawa when he joined the Foreign Service of Canada. We arrived in the city when I was expecting my first child. We rented a small apartment near the river, just above the E.B. Eddy factory, and the stink of that factory contributed more than a little to the dreadful morning, noon and night sickness that I endured.

In 1962, although far from being the rough sawmill town of the 1860s that Rosie Dunn knew, Ottawa was also far from being the vibrant, exciting, cultural city that it is now. Situated at the junction of two rivers and a canal, it still gave us lots of opportunities for boating and exploring. The Gatineau Hills across the Ottawa River afforded us with wonderful picnic spots — in spite of the inevitable blackflies and mosquitoes in the summer — and great skiing in the winter.

Although I was born in Toronto, and still love that city, Ottawa has always been special to me. During our thirty-four years in the Foreign Service, Ottawa was our home. We returned after every posting away to spend several years there. Every time we returned, we saw immense changes in the city. It grew, expanded and became the exciting and cosmopolitan metropolis that it is now, as we watched.

Writing this book has also been a great learning experience for me. When I was nine I moved with my parents to Argentina, and didn't return to Canada until it was time for me to go to university. I missed learning about Canadian history during those years, so doing the research for this book taught me a lot about my own country. It was fun too. In the interests of that research, I took a breathtaking trip in a modern jet boat through the Lachine Rapids. It was hard to imagine old-time paddlewheelers going through that wild water on purpose.

One of the hardest things to figure out was the schedule for Rosie's train trip from Québec City to Ottawa. I calculated the distance and worked out how long I thought it would have taken in 1866. Was I ever wrong! Luckily I was put in touch with a Mr. R.L. Kennedy, who makes a hobby of studying old-time train schedules. I found out from him that what takes around five hours nowadays would have taken more than a day, then.

Quick. Rewrite!

Canada is my home and it is an amazing country. I have thoroughly enjoyed digging deeper into the early years of its history and the history of the city that became its capital. Who would have ever believed that pigs once roamed the streets of Ottawa?

✥

Yet again, I would like to thank my editors, Sandra Bogart Johnston and Diane Kerner. They are unbelievably talented and painstaking. I appreciate their support and expertise more than I can say.

Thanks, also, to the staff of the National Library and Archives and the Bytown Museum in Ottawa. I spent many hours in both places. The assistance and resources I found there were invaluable.

Finally, I appreciate the meticulous fact checking of the text by Barbara Hehner and Dr. Ross Fair of Ryerson University. I am also indebted to R.L. Kennedy, who was able to provide me with schedules and routes of the trains in Québec and Ontario in 1866 and 1867.

Public Library

While the events described and some of the characters in this book
may be based on actual historical events and real people,
Rosie Dunn is a fictional character created by the author,
and her diary is a work of fiction.

Library and Archives Canada Cataloguing in Publication

Bradford, Karleen
A country of our own : the Confederation diary of Rosie
Dunn / by Karleen Bradford.

(Dear Canada)
Issued also in electronic format.
ISBN 978-1-4431-1324-3

1. Canada--History--Confederation, 1867--Juvenile literature.
I. Title. II. Series: Dear Canada

PS8553.R217C68 2013 jC813'.54 C2013-901793-3

6 5 4 3 2 1 Printed in Canada 114 13 14 15 16 17

First printing September 2013

Go to www.scholastic.ca/dearcanada for information on the
Dear Canada series — see inside the books, read an excerpt
or a review, post a review, and more.